# My Autobiography

# My Autobiography

DR. B. R. AMBEDKAR

*Published by*
**PRABHAT PRAKASHAN PVT. LTD.**
4/19 Asaf Ali Road,
New Delhi-110 002 (INDIA)
e-mail: prabhatbooks@gmail.com

ISBN 978-93-5562-762-9
**MY AUTOBIOGRAPHY**
*By* Dr. B. R. Ambedkar



*Edition*
2025

*Price*
₹ 450 (Rupees Four Hundred Fifty Only)

*Printed at*
R-Tech Offset Printers, Delhi

# About this Book

The autobiography of Dr. B.R. Ambedkar is a monumental work that traces his extraordinary life and indomitable spirit as one of India's greatest social reformers and visionaries. The life story of Dr. Bhimrao Ramji Ambedkar is one of great struggle, tenacity, and ongoing pursuit of equality and justice for the oppressed.

This intensive autobiography as it serves as a testament to the victory of the human spirit over adversity chronicles Dr. Ambedkar's challenges, ambitions, and accomplishment. His life story is more than just his own; it also serves as a mirror to reflect social, political, and economic landscape during one of India's most revolutionary times.

Born in a marginalised community, Dr. Ambedkar suffered the shackles of caste prejudice from a very young age. He nevertheless, became a bright scholar and a beacon of light for the oppressed and the poor thanks to his unyielding resolve and need for knowledge. He was motivated by his academic prowess and a strong sense of empathy to fight against the social injustice that was woven in the fabric of Indian society.

In this autobiography, Dr. Ambedkar takes us on a transformative journey through his early years, his fight against caste prejudice, his pursuit of education, and his unwavering pursuit of social justice and human rights. In addition to discussing his experiences as a student, lawyer, and scholar, he also shares his role as the primary architect of the Indian Constitution.

Through his deep insight, Dr. Ambedkar challenges social norms and exposes the injustice done to the marginalized communities and presents several measures for their emancipation. His vision for a just and equal society, free from shackles of caste discrimination resonates powerfully even today. He envisioned a society based on the principles of freedom, equality and fraternity, where every individual gets an equal opportunity to flourish and contribute towards the progress of the nation.

The autobiography of Dr. B.R. Ambedkar reminds us of the courage that challenged the deep-rooted systems of oppression. This shows the significant personal sacrifices and indecible impact of Dr. Ambedkar's enduring impact. His role as the chairman of the Drafting Committee of the Indian Constitution, where he worked relentlessly to protect every citizen's rights and dignity, is evidence of his unshakable commitment to social justice.

This edition of the autobiography has been presented with utmost devotion and care. The purpose is to disseminate Dr. Ambedkar's inspiring story among a larger audience. It pays homage to his enduring legacy, amazing accomplishments, and lifetime struggle. Through the pages of this book, the readers will learn more about the difficulties faced by the deprived communities, the value of education and empowerment, and the necessity of group action in the pursuit of a just and inclusive society.

Let us be motivated by Dr. BR Ambedkar's fortitude, brilliance, and unshakable commitment to the ideals of social justice as we begin our in-depth journey through his life. His narrative acts as a beacon, igniting in us a spirit of pathos, sympathy, and never-ending pursuit of equality.

❑

# Contents

# Am I Not That!

My grandfather's name was Malojirao. He had a younger brother, who had returned home after around 24 years since he joined the Sadhu Mandali, a group of ascetics, when he was around fourteen or fifteen years of age. My grandfather and great-grandmother were still alive at that time. She was ecstatic to see her son again. She urged the son to get married and settle down. My grandfather also persuaded the monk so. However, the younger brother refused to listen to either of them. Taking my grandfather aside, he said, "Brother, even after observing penance for so many years, I am not satisfied yet, therefore let me leave again now, don't plead me into getting married".

In response, my grandfather told him that he had no objections either. But, my great-grandmother was not ready to forgo her younger son. The monk then suggested a plan his older sibling to use a ruse to convince their mother. He said that, "This monk has come after all these years; what is the proof that he is your son? The sages and hermits also practise witchcraft. This monk might use the witchcraft to trick into grappling the home and property! Therefore, if the monk wants to leave, let him go, do not insist". My great-grandmother readily agreed after hearing this and the monk left.

The monk returned home exactly 20 years after this incident. However, at that time, my great-grandmother had already expired and her monk son had also become aged. Although, my grandfather made repeated requests to the monk to stay at home; however, he refused saying instead, "Brother, I have a little life left. I am here to meet with you people. We will not meet again. Please do not insist me to stay. However, as I go, I bless you that a Saviour will be born in your third generation who will liberate his third generation." After leaving such a fortunate message, the monk had gone forever.

I occasionally have the impression that I have an extremely sharp mind. So, as per the sage's prophecy, am I not the savour of third generation?

❑

# I was Born in Mool Nakshatra

Recalling the incidents of my past brings my childhood memories alive. I am turning sixty. But, I do not recall my birth date as no proof of the same exists. My parents did not consider it necessary, nobody kept the records. What's so special about childbirth? Why keep the date in mind? My parents might have thought in a similar way. They didn't make my Kundali (horoscope) even though my father had knowledge about astrology. He used to express promising thoughts about my future. He followed a regular daily routine. Therefore, I presume the date of birth submitted by my father to my school must be correct. When I was born my father was in the 7th Pioneer regiment. My parents were originally from Konkan, but they were settled in Mhow (Madhya Pradesh) in Central India at the time of my birth. Recalling a few clear incidents from my childhood, I believe I was born at 12 o'clock in midnight. Also, I was born in Mool Nakshatra. The family astrologer declared that since the child is born in Mool Nakshatra, this will lead to the death of his mother. My father paid no attention to this absurd prediction, yet my brothers and sisters began to despise me for sure. Everyone condemned me saying the boy is ominous for the family. It is surprising when childhood memories come to mind. I used to wear only langoti (loin cloth) till the age of 12. Going from door to door I chopped wood for other people, which I was fond of.

After my mother's death my aunt (father's younger brother's wife) brought me up. I worked as a gardener for six months. I had the habit of climbing trees like a monkey. And I used to hang the blanket on the tree and sleep on the swing itself. That tree was in front of our house. There was a heap of garbage under the tree. I won't climb down the tree, rather jump on the heap of garbage. A lot of ash would fly and stick to my body. Plague broke out in our village at that time. People point fingers at me and say - so many people die of plague, but why doesn't this one die? My aunt used to feel very bad. She would say to everyone "Don't say anything to the child!"

When my mother passed away in my childhood, I misused that freedom. Everyone used to say, "this boy is good for nothing". I regret that none of them is alive today. Their prediction would have proved wrong today.

I have also worked as an animal herdsman. I might have also turned into a shepherd. But my father felt that I should learn the art of working in the shade rather than splintering stones for a living. I have reached this stage today. Nobody should assume that the reason for this was I had innate merit. In fact, I worked hard to get where I am today.

My father was a Kabirpanthi monk and an education enthusiast. Dharmasana or Vidyasana would be the fitting name for my father's house. My father made me memorise the Ramayana, Mahabharata, and other epics by the time I was 12 years old. He was a devout man. Once I insisted to my aunt (mother's sister) that I would not attend school. "Aunty, you ask me to go to school. But what will happen if I go to school," I further continued. What answer the helpless aunt would have given? However, my father asserted that, "Drona was a Brahmin, still rose to become a famous warrior. We are poor, so why can't you study and be a scholar?" His words left a lasting impression on my mind.

❑

# Things My Father Taught Me

My father was a teacher. There was a good rule of the East India Company government. However, we can call this our misfortune that this rule was not continued further. The rule was that education was compulsory for the soldiers in the army of the Company Government. There was a day school for the soldiers' sons and daughters and a night school for the adults. Each platoon had an independent school for itself. My father was the headmaster of one such school for 14 years. There was a modest school in Pune to train good teachers for the benefit of soldiers. My father took training in that school and obtained a teacher's diploma. His way of teaching was very good. It is because of this that my father developed a passion and belief for education. The women folk and children of the house knew how to read and write very well. Not only this, because of my father, my sisters had acquired the ability to read books like Pandav Pratap and Ramayana and learned to comment on them. Being a Kabirpanthi himself, he remembered hymns and abhang verses.

My father wanted me to study Sanskrit. But my wish could not be fulfilled. The reason was that my elder brother was studying in fourth standard in Satara. He wanted to study Sanskrit and become a good scholar. But, the Sanskrit teacher refused to teach the language to the untouchable students. Because of the bigotry of the teacher, my brother was forced to take the Persian language. That teacher used to despise us in the class that discouraged us. When I reached the fourth standard, I was well aware of the ill-will of the Sanskrit teacher. As a result, I also had to opt for the Persian language. I am proud of Sanskrit language. Even today, I wish to learn the language well, to read and understand it completely. It is my heartily desire to achieve proficiency in Sanskrit language. I don't know when that day will come!

I studied the Persian language deeply. I used to secure 90-95 marks out of 100. Yet, it has to be admitted that the Persian literature pales in comparison to the Sanskrit literature. In Sanskrit literature, there is poetry, contemplation, ornamentation, drama; there are epics like Ramayana—Mahabharata. It has philosophy, mathematics, and logic. Sanskrit literature has everything from the point of view of modern education. However, that is not the case in Persian literature. I am proud of Sanskrit language. I had a strong desire to know that language well. However, due to the narrow and conservative attitude of the teacher, I had to alienate myself from Sanskrit.

The atmosphere of the house was disciplined because of my father. He was a soldier and his strict discipline sometimes became a cause of annoyance. But today I feel bad. If I had worked as hard as my father wished, it was not impossible for me to get a second division in the Bombay University examination. I did not understand the meaning of father's concern for me at that time. We used to think that our father unnecessarily pressurised us for studies.

My father was very fond of mathematics. He had solved all the examples of Gokhale's Arithmetic and saved them in a large notebook in beautiful handwriting. He wanted me to study those maths tricks from time to time and acquire mastery in the subject so that I could pass with good grades. No one would believe how much he cared for me.

We came to Bombay for English education where I was enrolled in Maratha High School. Earlier the condition of our house was fine, but later it became pathetic. At that time my father was getting a meagre pension and in such a situation he was living in Mumbai with a family consisting of several members. On top of that my father used to bring me books of my choice. It was all beyond the scope of my father. Despite enduring all this he was always ready to provide me with all the comforts. When I remember these things, I feel very proud of my father. My heart tells me that very few sons have such a kind father. I could not understand the value of my dear father's ideals at that time due to my carefree nature.

I was fond of reading other books since earlier times thus neglecting my studies. My Father did not like my carelessness. He used to tell me to finish school studies first and then read other books. Just as father was proud of Marathi language, he was also proud student of English language. He was also very fond of teaching English. He always asked me to memorise Harward's book in front of him.

Accordingly, I memorised three books of Tarkhadkar's translation course. My father had taught me the art of finding the proper English equivalent of the Marathi language words and using it at the appropriate place. I speak and write good English. Such is my reputation, I guess. However, no teacher taught me the way my father taught me to use right words at the right places. He used to test my knowledge by asking wrong words from Tarkhadkar's book. Likewise, he has taught me to form correct English sentences and use of proper language style.

❑

# I Was Incredibly Special

To have one's own book collection means to have one's own property; such was the ambition of that time. With the same ambition, my Granth Sangrahalay has been made at present. I used to go to my father to fetch new books at that time. It never happened that I asked for a book and my father did not bring that book till evening! Our financial condition was very pathetic. However, I was not even aware of this at that time. My father had a big heart. Mostly, I didn't have money in my pocket to buy books. But whenever I requested one, my father got me that book. He would take his stole and come out. At that time both my married sisters were living in Bombay. My father used to go straight to the younger sister first. She hardly had three - four rupees with her from the savings! The poor woman used to sadly say that, "I don't have that much money." From there my father would go straight to the elder sister. If he did not get the money from her either, he would mortgage some of their jewelry (given to my sisters in marriage). And after getting the pension, the father would go to the Marwari's place and retrieve the jewelry back for my sisters. As a result, my sisters never refused to share their jewelry to help my father whenever he asked for them.

My mother had passed away when I was very young. I was raised by my father's sister. Being elder to my father, my Aunt had control over the family. My father also used to respect her a lot because of which I was also dear to my aunt. As a result other members of the family also did not say anything to me. Because of this I was loved even more in the family. My father endured every suffering for my happiness and peace; but I was oblivious of this situation. I used to apply a lot of oil on my head and would sleep peacefully by making a pillow of new books. You can imagine the plight of these books! I was so fond of reading since childhood that I can tell in which book, at which place, which important idea is there even now. My memory is very sharp because of this habbit.

❑

# My Father

Despite being poor, the environment at our house was like that of a progressive, well-educated family. My father was always careful that our character should be pure and that we develop interest in education. He used to take us to the temple in the morning before having food and used to recite bhajans, couplets, abhangs. I hesitated to perform all these acts. After reciting two or four abhangs somehow, I would sit near the food plate. Then my father would ask, 'Why did the bhajans end early today?' I used to disappear from there before I could answer his question. However, father didn't let this mischief go on at all. At eight in the night my sisters, my elder brother, and I had to be at the temple. Such was his strict rule. Father would not forgive anyone who were absent. Father used to listen to Abhangs of saints and couplets of Kabir with great devotion. This used to create a holy and soulful atmosphere all around. Our father used to do all this from the heart. We wondered a lot. My sisters also used to recite Abhang in a melodious voice. At that time I used to think how much religion and education of religion is necessary for human life.

Many people think that I am religious. But this is not true. This thinking of theirs is not correct. Those who have shared my company know well about my devotion and love for religion. I don't like showing off at all. It is my opinion that, "The religion whose teachings do not free man from his animal instincts, that religion is useless". My views are progressive. The credit for this goes to the religious nature of my father. He sowed the seed of the path of devotion in my mind in my childhood itself. Our father made us read religious books like Ramayana, Mahabharata etc. in our childhood. No one dared to ask that, 'Why are we compelled to read Ramayana-Mahabharata?' I used to think why do we need to know the biographies of the beings mentioned in Puranas wherein the Shudras and the untouchables are being neglected at every step?

There is no one else as religious as me. I asked my father, "What is the need of reading these scriptures?" I did not understand this clearly. By the path of devotion man becomes a worshiper of power and an idolater; and this is a huge flaw. That's why this path of devotion is dangerous for the nation. This is my authentic opinion. Perhaps my views will not be acceptable to the people. However, people should consider my statement as well as its diachronic role with an unbiased mind. An intellectual will find my words appropriate. Man should learn to think rationally as well as humanely. Because of my father, I got by heart the compositions of poets like Tukaram, Mukteshwar etc. Not only this, I started thinking about those poems in my mind. There would be very few people to study so many Marathi saint poets. I love languages and I know English well; at the same time I am proud of Marathi language. For many years I was the editor of magazines like 'Mooknayak', 'Bahishkrit Bharat', 'Janata Pakshik' etc. I have written a lot in Marathi. I have also studied German language well. I have somewhat forgotten this language (German) now; but hopefully I can read it again after a few days of effort. You know that day before yesterday I gave a speech in Gujarati in Ahmedabad. At first I was afraid to give lectures in Marathi, but later I realised that I can speak Marathi very well. I also know French language.

Let me tell you some more important things about my father. My father got the idea that I should do B.A. I used to get up at two in the night to study. It is my belief that at that time the mind remains calm and happy, and therefore one can study properly. I had to get up at two o'clock in the night at the time of examination; therefore, my father would not sleep till two o'clock in the night. I used to grumble angrily when my father would wake me up to study. A lamp was kept by the head. I wondered, how much light would it give and how much would I read in its light? Somehow I would lie on the side of the lamp studying or pretending to study till five in the morning. I was not allowed to lie in bed after five in the morning. I used to often tell my father, "I never fail. I pass every year. But still why do you keep pestering me to study?"

There were good professors like Oswald Müller, Principal Caverton, Prof. George Andersen in our Elphinstone College. But, they did not create any enthusiasm in my mind. Müller loved me very much. He used to give me his shirts and books. Yet, this is equally true that his teachings could not evoke new consciousness in my mind. I kept passing the exam in college, but failed to secure second rank. In under-graduation, I failed to secure second rank by few marks. Given the progress of my studies at that time, the degrees that I obtained later on and the many books that I wrote, could anyone have predicted that I would be able to achieve all this?

❑

# Bitter Experience

I was born in Mhow (Indore). At that time my father was working in the Army. He was a Subedar in the Army. For our living in the Army cantonment, we had no contact with the outside world; because of which I had no idea about the prevalence of untouchability. However, when my father retired, we all started living in Satara. When I was five years old, my mother passed away. When the famine struck Goregaon in Satara district, the government started the relief work. They started the work of constructing a pond. My father was appointed to pay wages to the labourers on the construction site of the pond. He himself went to Goregaon and made us stay back in Satara. After coming here, we started sensing 'untouchability' in real sense. First there was no barber available to shave our beards. We had to face many difficulties. At that time my elder sister used to shave all four of us brothers. For the first time, I understood why we were treated so even after the availability of many barbers in Satara.

My father lived in Goregaon. He wrote letters to us. Once he sent us a letter inviting us to Goregaon. I was very happy that we would go to Goregaon by train. Till then I had not even seen a train. With the money sent by father we bought nice clothes and we all went to Goregaon to meet my father. Prior to this we had sent him a letter; but due to the carelessness of the servant, the letter could not reach him. We got down the train and started looking for the servant; but we were disappointed. My guise made me look like a Brahmin. The train had left. We waited at the station for more than half an hour. But there was nobody at the station except us. At the same time, seeing us children, the station master came to us and asked - 'Where are you going? Who are you?' The station master was startled as soon as we uttered the word 'Mahar'. He took ten steps back. However, seeing our attire he thought that we are the children of some rich Mahar. He assured us of providing ox cart. But till seven in the evening the ox carts were not ready to give ride to the children of the Mahars. Finally a coachman agreed, but on the condition that he would not drive the cart. I had spent many days in the army cantonment, so I had no problem in driving an ox cart.

As soon as we gave our consent, the coachman brought the cart and we left for Goregaon. We found a canal at some distance from the village. The coachman said, "You people eat here; you won't find water ahead." We got down for eating. But the water of the canal was very dirty. It was contaminated with cow dung. The coachman went to another place and came back after diving. We again continued with our journey on the ox cart. It was late in the night. There was neither the lamp nor any man on the way. We all cried a lot. Somehow it clocked twelve midnight! On the other hand, many thoughts were coming in my mind. We thought that we would not be able to reach Goregaon. Meanwhile, as soon as we reached Tolnaka, we got down from the cart. I asked the man sitting at the Tolnaka about a place to eat. I knew Russian and hence I did not face any difficulty conversing with him. But he said nonchalantly, "There will be water on the mountain ahead." Somehow we spent the night at Tolnaka and reached Goregaon dead-tired by ox cart the next afternoon.

❑

# It Is Well Known

Being a Kabirpanthi, my father did not consume meat, fish, alcohol etc. He was a pure vegetarian and did not even touch alcohol. However, whenever there was a caste-based feast in our village, my father used to take initiative to provide sweets and non-vegetarian food to everyone. In our traditional household, we had big utensils for cooking and serving, which were used in the village public feast. My father himself used to go to the village and collect big stones under the tree and prepare big stoves for cooking. Delicious food was prepared from fish, chicken and goat meat and father particularly took the charge of cooking. He didn't see anything wrong with this leadership. He used to say, 'we did not eat what was cooked.' Thus, he followed his liberal philosophy. Not only this, he used serve alcohol, in small quantities, to people gathered for community lunch. However, he had not touched even a drop of alcohol in his entire life time. I have followed this tradition too. When I was on the Viceroy's Executive Board, I treated my friends to delicious food along with whiskey and champagne. And this is well known, like my father, I too have never touched a drop of alcohol.

❑

# I Learned This

I have already told that I was a normal student till BA. I didn't expect any improvement at my own hands and neither did others expect it from me. It's not that I was a dull mind or uninterested in my studies; but revision requires a special kind of approach. Or it could also be that due to lack of necessary guidance from the professors, my mental power could not progress properly. Despite born with congenital qualities a man needs to develop them over the time. I accept that, by the time I moved to America, my qualities were dormant and developed only in company of learned Professor Seligman and other scholars. Being in the company of these learned professors I felt that I have become capable of thinking independently. Once I asked Professor Seligman how should I revise. He said, "You continue your work. Then you will automatically understand how revision should be done."

While writing a book, one does not notice how the time passes and how the days pass one after the other. All my energy gets concentrated while writing. I don't care about food. Sometimes, I stay up all night reading and writing. At that time I feel neither tired nor lazy. But when the work is over, I feel frustrated and unsatisfied. I got troubles in life, but could not get as much happiness as I got on the publication of my book.

❑

# Father's Death

After finishing BA, my father wanted me to stay back in Bombay and not go to Baroda. My father had already anticipated the humiliation I would face after reaching Baroda. He tried to convince me in different ways that I should not look for job in Baroda. But I did not give up my insistence and went to Baroda. Suddenly, I got a telegram about his illness in Baroda. I left for Bombay from Baroda. I got down at Surat railway station to get ice cream for my father on the way; and unfortunately as a result of that I missed the train. There was no option but to wait for the next train. Consequently, I reached Bombay late the next day. When I came home, I saw that my father was on the verge of death. Everyone was sitting by his bed side worrying. My heart ached seeing that scene. My father lovingly caressed my head, looked at me with tears in his eyes, and left this world. I seemed that he was holding on to his breath just to see me one last time. I am very sorry that I could not meet my father earlier because I had gotten down at Surat.

❑

# Tenacious Nature

I was of the stubborn nature earlier. However, I will not be able to tell for sure whether it is the same now or not. Let me tell you about my childhood. I was studying English in class II. Our school was in Satara Camp. Pendse Guruji used to teach us. He loved me very much. I had a very stubborn nature and my classmates knew it. They knew that I would certainly do something if I am told not to do it. Once, it was raining heavily. By that time it was time for us to go to school. My friends said that, "Look it is raining heavily. Don't go to school otherwise you will get wet." I was waiting for this opportunity. My elder brother came out with an umbrella. I told him, "you go alone with an umbrella, I will follow you drenched."

My brother pestered me a lot but I did not agree. And I left home without umbrella. At that time I used to wear a cap with leaves and flowers. I handed over the cap to my brother and followed him to the school in the rain. When I reached school, I was completely drenched. Guru ji saw me in this condition.

He felt very sorry. He asked me, "Hey, why didn't you bring an umbrella in the heavy rain?" I replied, “There was only one umbrella. We two brothers have only one umbrella! That's why I came soaking wet.” Actually I told a lie. This thing did not come to the attention of Guruji. He called my elder brother, who was studying in the fourth standard. Guruji asked him, "Tell me, how many shirts you are wearing?" The brother replied, "I am wearing only one shirt." Then Guru ji sent me along with his son to his house and told the son, “Take him home and bathe him with warm water. Give him a loincloth to wear and also dry his clothes so that by evening he can go home wearing those clothes.”

Accordingly, Guruji’s son took me home and bathed me in warm water and gave me a loincloth to wear. I was ecstatic; at least, I had freedom from school till evening. I wandered outside the school whistling. “Why didn’t I come to class?” Guru ji wondered! Guruji sent a student to look for me. I was ashamed to sit in the class in a loincloth. Then Guruji said, “Hey, all are students here, therefore you should not feel shy from anyone.” I sat in the class crying. I was very embarrassed. It was then that I decided to jilt my stubborn nature. I leave it on others to tell that to what extent I was able to achieve this resolution.

Our surname was not ‘Ambedkar’. Our correct surname is ‘Ambewadekar’. Five miles away near Dapoli in Khed tehsil there is a village named Ambewade. That was why people identified us by the name Ambewadekar. How did Ambewadekar become Ambedkar also has a history. I had a Brahmin teacher with surname Ambedkar. He did not teach us much. But he had great affection for me. During noon break I had to walk a long distance to my home for food. Guruji did not like this. But I had only this much time for fun so I loved to go home. But Guruji thought a solution. He would bring home cooked food with him to the school and invite me in lunch break to share the same. He dropped roti and vegetables on my hands lest I should touch him.

I take pride in saying that the taste of those roti-vegetables given with love was outlandish. Remembering this incident make my heart heavy. Actually, Ambedkar Guruji had a lot of affection for me.

One day Guruji said to me, "It is difficult to pronounce the name Ambewadekar; instead Ambedkar is a good name. You must add this as your surname." And then, he also entered the same in the school register as well. While I was going to London for the Round Table Conference, he had sent me a very affectionate letter. That letter is still there in my collection. If in future I wrote my autobiography (character), I would publish that letter. There was something different in the nature of Ambedkar Guruji. He used to come to the class as soon as the school bell rang.

There was a senior student named Rahimtullah in our class. Entrusting all the responsibility on him Guruji would go out of class. There was much difference between age of Rahimtullah and other students of the class. Our age was 10-12 years, whereas Rahimtullah's was 25-30 years! Guruji used to come to the class before the school closed in the evening and ask Rahimtullah, "How are you? Did the children misbehave?" Rahimtullah would answer by saying, "No". Then Guruji would go home reassured. You will ask where did Guruji go all day. There was a small shop of peppermint, cigarettes etc. in front of our school. The watchman and the students used to buy goods from that shop, and thus, the shop ran well. Leaving the school Guruji would go to the shop where he kept the shop's accounts. He earned 20-25 rupees per month from this work.

The trouble for Guruji increased when the officials came to school for the annual examinations. When the officers asked mathematics questions, Guruji would write answer on a slate and show us secretly from the adjoining room. All students would get the answers right and the officials used to glorify Guruji for his excellent teaching. At the end of the exam Guruji used to get excellent comments in the visit book. Officers were treated with tea, breakfast, and cigar. After getting one good comment Guruji would get free to write accounts for the whole year.

❑

# Your Condition

There were established rules during the Peshwa era regarding who should wear what. My mother used to tell us that when Mahars went to buy cloths, the shopkeeper would show the items from the shop itself, and the price had to be asked from a distance. Following the purchase of clothing, it was soaked in water before being rubbed into the mud, because untouchables should only not wear new clothes. They should wear old, torn clothing. It was necessary to split the filthy saree into two halves. Eventually, the Mahars had to keep the money there and then had to take the cloth. The loincloth that we wore was the order issued by the Peshwa. The non-Brahmins wore dhotis with pleats on only one side, while the Brahmins wore them with pleats on both sides. The Bhandari people would tie a scarf around their waist and wrap a large part of it around the waist, such was the rule.

When the British government took over, Bombay went under their control. Peshwas had their sharp eyes on the goldsmiths. Both the Peshwas and the goldsmiths claim that they were

Brahmins. The goldsmiths used to wear dhotis like those of Brahmins. Peshwas didn't want them to wear dhoti in Brahmin style. The Peshwas began to allege that the British had drowned the religion. The British got angry with this. British officers heard Peshwa's pleas. The Peshwa alleged that, "We placed prohibitions on people. Under your rule, those people are now seen wearing dhotis from behind." The East India Company was new here. There were moneylenders in Balkeshwar. On the complaint, the Chief Officer called the moneylenders and inquired about the allegations.

The goldsmiths were wearing dhotis tucking them behind. The Chief Officer deliberated on the complaint of Peshwas and instructed goldsmiths to stop donning the dhoti in the manner of Peshwas. They were levied a fine of 50 rupees by the Panchas too. People now dress up in a coat and trousers.

What did Mahars do then? They used to keep vigil in the night. They ate whatever leftover piece of bread was available in the morning. There was a Mahar in Phaltan village, who owned 24 bighas of land. The village had a temple. There a langar (community meal) was organised from time to time. The affluent Mahar had a minister. The langar received one cart of roti, laddoos and jalebi. The Mahars would eat food sitting near the temple. Having got this much, what do the Mahars need the land for? After going without food for a few days, the Mahars would say, "The Marathas have taken so much of our land." After performing Shradh at Jalgaon, the Mahars used to sit like beggars on the heap of garbage. The people wondered, "If he becomes a Christian, how will it be good for him?"

For thousands of years till the day before yesterday not even a single person of their community could become a graduate or a scholar. I see no harm in telling this fact. In my school, there was a house-keeper lady. She was a Maratha by caste. She never touched me. My mother used to tell me that "Address an elder man by calling him Mama (uncle / maternal uncle)." I used to call the postman as uncle. Once when I was in primary school I got thirsty. I told my teacher that I was thirsty. The teacher called the peon and said to him, "Take him to the tap". We went to the tap. I drank the water once the peon turned on the tap on. Otherwise, I could not drink water in school for days together, as I was not permitted to touch the tap.

Everyone might not be proud of their birthplace, but they do love it. After becoming pensioner, my father started living in Dapoli permanently. I began my studies in Dapoli. At the age of 5-6 years, driven by circumstances we had to leave the foothills of the mountains. My life till date has been spent mostly on the ghats / mountains. I came down from a ghat after 25 years. Anyone will be delighted to step into a state bathed in beauty. Happiness doubles for those who regard this state as their motherland. It would not be an exaggeration to say that at one time there was a situation when this area was on the path to progress from the point of view of untouchable caste. This state was full of untouchable caste officials at that time. Similarly the outcaste class was far ahead in education in comparision to other castes.

The job with the army was an important reason for this progress. To what extent the untouchables could have been happy before the British rule? Nothing can be said about it for sure today. But, the sense of untouchability was so strong at that time that the untouchables had to walk at a distance from the upper caste people so that even their shadow should not fall on the upper castes people while walking. Furthermore, the untouchables had to tie a black thread on their wrists for their identification. Opportunities were rare for these people at that time. Wherever the British set their feet in this country, the untouchables got an opportunity to raise their heads. Taking advantage of this opportunity they proved their physical courage, how vigorous they are, and how sharp they are intellectually. It has been proved that only progressive Brahmins or similar castes of that time curse us today by calling us untouchables, but other than our class everyone else was very progressive.

Therefore, we were enjoying authority and power in Konkan's Dapoli region. Job in the army gave us an opportunity to improve our living standard. Resultantly, we are not even an iota less in patience, intelligence, and cleverness etc. We were recruited on the post of officers in the army based only on our merits. The untouchables were appointed as headmasters in the army cantonment schools during this period. Since primary education was made compulsory in the army cantonment, therefore, it had relative impact on our lives. But, the British government betrayed us by closing the doors of the army for Mahar caste.

I have also taken birth from the womb of Mahar mother. If seen from the point of view of poverty, it is not that I had better facilities than today's poor students.

I have studied under the kerosene lamp (Rakheel) of one paisa while staying in a 10 feet room of Bombay's DD Chawl where I was living with my parents, and siblings. This is not all, if I could have achieved all this while facing all those difficulties and troubles, then any person could have become a scholar by just working hard. No one is intelligent by birth. While living in England as a student, I have successfully completed a course with the actual duration of 8 years in just 2 years and 3 months. For this I had to study for 21 hours out of 24 hours. Today I am 40 years of age, yet I work continuously sitting for 18 hours out of 24 hours. Present day youth feel the need to sniff the tapkir (tobacco) or smoke a cigarette after sitting continuously for half an hour. I never felt the need for any such thing even at this age.

It is not wrong to say that this job with the army brought a revolution in the Hindu society. In the village where on one hand, the Mahars and the charmakars (skinners) were not touched by the Marathas, and the Marathas considered it as an insult if the Mahars and the charmakars do not greet or salute to them (say Ram-Ram). On the other hand, the Maratha soldiers of the army used to bow before Mahars and skinners Subedars of the same army. Even if these Subedars said "Hey you", then these soldiers lacked the courage to raise their heads and look at the Subedar. The untouchable caste people here had so many rights which were not available to the same caste in any other province of the country. 10 per cent of the people among them were literate. It is noteworthy that not only the men of these caste were educated, but the women were also educated. Some women were so accomplished in learning that they used to make commentaries on the Puranas in the gathering of the men.

As long as the education continued, the untouchables gained a lot of benefits from it. They were very proud of the way they utilized their education. This statement would not be an exaggeration that because of this spread of knowledge, the collection of books among the untouchables was very large in terms of numbers. The handwritten copies of Sridhar Swami's book could be found in the vehicles. However, with many untouchables I have seen handwritten copies of ancient and great poets of Maharsashtra like Mukudam Raj, Gyaneshwar and Mukteshwar etc. Not only this, I believe that even today some rare treatises could be found in the homes of untouchables.

Very few people know that Gyaneshvara Maharaj had composed a treatise called "Panchikaran". But, I have seen this book at the house of my late friend. An advertisement was published in 'Kesari' that, "Mr. Pangarkar ji's kindly suggest that if anyone has a book titled "Gyan Sudha" written by Raghavchintan Dhan Kavi' a few years ago. If he had not found a handwritten copy of this book, then it could be found in the collection of my untouchable friend. The people from the untouchable caste, who were deprived of the education at that time, had to suffer a lot at that time, and this is also considerable what amount of money might have been spent in collecting such a book? Such longing for knowledge makes the society of that time proud.

❑

# Meeting with Maharaja Sayajirao Gaekwad

I had a meeting with Guruvarya Keluskar Guruji along with the King Sayajirao Gaekwad of Baroda at the Royal Palace in Bombay for the purpose of higher education.

Maharaj - Which subject do you want to study?

Bhimrao – Maharaj, Sociology, Economics and Public Finance.

Maharaj - What would you do next after studying these subjects?

Bhimrao – I will find out the way as to how can I improve the condition of my society by studying these subjects. And will bring social reforms using those solutions.

Maharaj - But you are going to do our work. Then how will it be possible for you to study, do a job and also do social service?

Bhimrao - If Maharaj gives me such an opportunity, I will organise all these works.

Maharaj - Bhimrao, I am thinking of sending you to America, are you ready to go?

Bhimrao - Yes Maharaj!

Maharaj - Then go to the education officer and apply for scholarship to study abroad and then tell me.

I went to America and received higher education after getting scholarship from the Baroda Government. I got a job with the princely state of Baroda as per the scholarship contract after I returned from America. However, I could not find any house to live in Baroda. Neither the Hindus nor the Muslims were ready to rent me any place to live. At last, I made up my mind to stay in a Parsi hospice as a Parsi. Eventually, I adopted the Parsi name of "Edalji Sorabji".

On the other hand, the word spread among the public that Maharaj had brought an educated Mahar youth to Baroda. People suspected that I was living secretly in hospice disguised as a Parsi. My secrecy was exposed. The Parsis came to know that I was the Mahar living in the hospice. The next day I left for the office after lunch. Meanwhile, 15-20 Parsis came with cudgels in their hands and asked, "Who are you?" I said, "I am a Hindu." They were not satisfied with this answer. My mind was thinking very fast at that time. I fearlessly asked them for eight hours' time. I tried to find a place to live elsewhere throughout the day. But, I could not find a place to live anywhere. I approached several of my friends, but, they turned away giving various excuses. In the end, I was so upset that I was not in a condition to understand anything. At last I sat near a tree and tears flowed down from my eyes. Eventually, I had to leave my job in Baroda and was forced to take the night train to Bombay.

❑

# Professor in Law College

I was a professor at Bombay's Sydenholm College from the year 1918 to the year 1920. I was also a Professor and the Principal in a law college. I severed my connection with the students since 1937. As a result, I left the professorship and entered politics. It is not enough to be a professor to just a scholar, but he should be multidimensional. His speech should be pure. He must be self driven. He ought to have the skill to present his subject in a captivating way, only then will enthusiasm be evoked among the students. Some qualities are innate while some qualities have to be acquired through experience and learning.

I had made some rules myself for checking the answer sheets of the students. I allotted 50 per cent marks for the overall gist of the answer and 50 per cent marks for the style, which included language writing, style of writing answers etc. My principle was to pass every student. Initially I used to allot at least 33 per cent marks. But when thousands of answer sheets came to me for checking I had to decide how many marks should be given. In such a situation, first I used to read the entire booklet, and then I give marks. I used to carefully read the copies which score more than 45 marks.

So, did the Hindu students not secure more than 45 per cent marks?

I have given 60 per cent marks to some students, though the numbers of such students was very less. I used to examine the copy thoroughly while giving 60 per cent marks.

Has any student got more than 60 per cent marks?

I have given more than 60 per cent marks to the students who deserved to obtain such high marks. They have this right. I recall an incident of that time. I gave 144 marks out of 150 to a student. In fact his answer sheet was worth it. He had written very good and intelligent answers. I felt that he should be given 150 marks. However, I gave six marks less because it was not a mathematical answer. Following which I sent that answer sheet to the official of the degree college. The officer noticed that the student of another college was scoring first position and that college would get the medal. Hence the officer sent that answer sheet to me for rechecking. But I did not make any changes. That answer sheet was sent to several examiners. Some gave less than 144 marks and some gave more than 144 marks. Finally, my assessment was made valid.

Have I failed any student?

It is impossible to tell whether I have caused any harm to a student or not.

Have I recommended a student? How was my behaviour at that time?

Once the guardian of an untouchable student found out that I was an examiner with the Bombay University. Hence, he approached me and began to recommend that student. He felt that being an untouchable, I would be able to help that student. But it was impossible for me. I see such recommendations with disdain. I told him, 'I can do that, but it will not be like a disgrace for me. Why should an educated untouchable youth consider himself insignificant, inferior and lowly in comparison to other educated youth? I want that the untouchable student should prove himself to be a better student as compared to the other students'. Listening to my reply, the gentleman silently left.

❑

# Mother, Have Arrived!

Dr. Ambedkar stopped at Satara ground. Halting at that place, he said, "Mother, I have arrived" and started crying. After sometime he told his friend, Dattoba Pawar, who was standing beside him, “These are the mortal remains of my mother. Mother has suffered a lot for us brothers and sisters. We have lived in that dilapidated house for some time that is visible on that side. My mother and brother used to work. I used to play a lot in the forest during my childhood. It is very painful for me that today my parents are not alive to see me.

❑

# Liveliness of Education

Ramabai: You have got a job for Rs. 450. That is enough for us. Quit the insistence for further studies. It would be good if you pay attention to the household.

Dr. Ambedkar: I will remarry if you start causing obstacles in my studies. How would an illiterate woman like you would know the importance of education?

Ramabai : Go, marry as many times as you want, but I will not let anyone step into my house.

Both Dr. Ambedkar and Ramabai started laughing.

Rama, the children of our community leave their parents and stay in the hostel. They get sweet dishes there to eat, but not mutton. Therefore, we will serve mutton in the Shradhdh. If you don't cook, I will take the children to the hotel and have them eat there.

Ramabai wondered, 'I had desire to serve puran roti (sweet flat bread) but had to surrender to my husband's insistence and I fed mutton to 50-60 children.'

# Familial Letter

Greetings dear Ramu,

I received your letter. I am very sad to read that Gangadhar is ill. Everything is a matter of time. Worrying about it will not do any good.

It is a matter of great pleasure to know that your studies are going well. I am in financial trouble here. There's nothing to send you, yet I am trying to make some arrangement for you. It is taking time. Sell the jewelry if you have run out of money. I will get you new jewelry when I come there.

How are Yashwant's and Mukund's studies going? You have not written anything in the letter. Don't worry about me my health is fine. My studies are still going on. I will not be able to come till June. I will tell about this later.

There is no news about Sakhu and Manjula. When you get the money, buy a saree each for Manjula and Lakshmi's mother. What is news about Shankar? How is Gajra?

Best wishes for all,

Bhimrao

❑

# The Greatness of Dr. Ambedkar

Dr. Ambedkar was about to be awarded the title of D.Sc. in London. A felicitation ceremony was being organised in Bombay in this regard. The handbills of the ceremony were prepared, in which it was written, 'Sir, will come with the title of D.Sc. from the foreign country.'

Dr. Ambedkar saw that handbill and told the people angrily that 'I have not yet received the title. The result for the title will be out in two-three months. It is not appropriate to take the task in your hands without knowing the actual facts. In fact, you should have asked for my consent first. You have organised the meeting without my consent and also released handbills. What message will go to the people? They will think that I have asked you to do all this, that I am eager to get the certificate. Even the upper caste people would say, "Look, Mahar has gone to England, has received higher education from there and is asking for salutations from his own people".'

I have received education, this does not mean that I have done something of great pride. What work have I done for the society to get the letter of honour from the society? You can give the letter of honour whenever I do any concrete work for the society. I will gladly accept it. At present, I am unable to accept this citation.

❑

# Duologue Between Husband and Wife

Dr. Babasaheb Ambedkar had received a fee for winning the case. He placed the money in front of Ramabai when he came home and said, "Take this money! I do not look at the world, I do not look at my wife. You always keep chanting my name. Count it and tell me that how much is this amount?"

Ramabai made eleven bundles of twenty rupee notes and said that these are eleven!

Babasaheb got a little annoyed and said – "What is the total amount of money?"

Ramabai laughed and said – "You know how much the amount is. You count thousands of rupees, but I do not know how to count. Am I an educated woman?"

Both started laughing.

After that Babasaheb said, "It is alright that you are this illiterate woman, otherwise you would have annoyed me a lot!"

❑

# Books and Home

(Dr. Babasaheb Ambedkar had bought five parts of the book 'Loss of England' for Rs. 500 and started reading it diligently at home).

Ramabai served the food. Saheb (Ambedkar) was engrossed in reading. Seeing this, Ramabai interrupted him 6-7 times for food.

Babasaheb: "Why are you repeating the same thing again? I bought these books for Rs. 500. Let me finish this page, then I'll eat."

"Tell me this much, then have food. Is it written on that page that a husband should pay attention to his wife, children and household?" Saheb smiled and then started eating.

"You always say that I do not pay attention towards the world. So what should I do?''

Ramabai said, "A household uses vegetables, oil, and salt. The husband should pay attention there. He should accept the children with love. He should speak a few words with his wife too. Your books and you! They come and go. What was the need to spend 500 rupees for books? A new guest (child) is going to come to your house in a few days. Is this an imagination?"

Next day Babasaheb brought six-seven sacks of vegetables and 100-125 dried fish (bombil). Seeing this, Ramabai said, "Devaji! These vegetables will wither in a day or two. We cannot cook it all today itself!"

❑

# Death of Rajratna

Dear Dattoba,

I suddenly received your letter today. Shivtarkar had written about the demise of my son after a long time. However, I have not received any reply from you. I thought that you have stopped to think about me. However, it is not the case. The comfort that you have extended to me in the times of my grief and sorrow is the proof that the flame has not gone off yet.

There is no use pretending that my wife and I recover from the shock of my son's death and I do not think that we ever can. Till now we have entombed in all four precious children, three sons and a daughter. We get sad whenever we remember them. Their world would have been very different had they been alive. The vision we had created had all been destroyed. The clouds of sorrow have been flowing through our lives. With the loss of our kids the salt of our life, that brings the taste to the life, is gone. It has been said in the Bible that, "Ye are the salt of the cart, if it leaveth the earth wherewith shall it be salted?"

The truth of these words is evident from my blank life. My last son was an abnormal one. Hardly have I seen any other child like him. With his passing away life to me has become like a deserted garden. It is not possible for me to write any further in this time of sorrow.

Your dreary friend,
B. R. Ambedkar

❑

# Water of Chavdar Reservoir of Mahad - Satyagrah

**Kolaba District Excommunicated Council**

## First Session - Mahad

19, 20 March, 1927

This council was organized in Mahad on Saturday 19th March and Sunday 20th March. More than three thousand untouchables participated in the council. In which Gangadhar Neelkanth Sahasrabuddhe, Anant Vinayak Chitre, Sitaram Namdev Shivtarkar, Balram Ambedkar, Pandurang Rajbhoj, Shantaram Upsham, More, Ramchandra Shinde, Dhondiram Gaikwad, Shivram Jadhav etc were present.

Proceedings began on 19 March 1927 at 5 pm. In the beginning, Sambhaji Tukaram Gaikwad, the chairman of the reception committee, welcomed the guests and introduced the council. After getting the information and approval as per the rules, the chairman of the council Dr. Bhimrao, Ramji Ambedkar, M.A., Ph.D., D.Sc. Bar at Law began with the speech –

Gentlemen, I am grateful to you for the honour you have bestowed on me today. I was requested to accept the chairmanship of this council. As is my nature, I was in favour of quitting the post. However, I could not avoid it. Because I had done this, the people present here would have been very angry with me. Therefore, I accepted this responsibility without any hesitation and today I am standing before of you.

I am very happy to be here today. Even if someone is not proud of his place of birth, there is definitely love. After my father began to receive his pension, he came to live in Dapoli permanently. My studies started at Dapoli school itself. My life was spent in the hilly region from the age of five till yesterday. I have come down from the hills after twenty five years today. This region is very prosperous from the point of view of natural beauty. In midst of this place, not just me, anyone will be happy. My happiness has doubled after coming here. But, I have no hesitation in saying so that on this occasion I am feeling both sad as well as happy. It would not be an exaggeration to say that there was a time when the people of this region were very progressive. This area was replete with officials from untouchable caste at that time. As compared to other communities, the untouchable community, except a few white-collar people, had progressed far ahead in the field of education.

The main reason for the progress of the untouchable society was their employment in the army. The life of the untouchables was no less than any hell before the arrival of the British in India. The untouchability was at its peak. The untouchables had to take longer walks so that their shadows did not touch the people from the upper castes. Their spitting profaned the road, hence they had to hang a pot on neck. The untouchables had to tie a black thread on their wrists to reveal their identity.

The untouchables of this state got a chance to hold their heads high and look at other people when the British stepped on the soil of this country. Taking advantage of the opportunity the people of this region proved their bravery, acumen and intelligence. If anyone wants a proof of this, they should read the Army registers. Several Subedars, Jamadars and Havaldars have come from the untouchable class of this state. Several became the headmaster after passing out from general school. Several proved their responsibility by becoming the accounts clerks and quarter master, clerks. My speech would be longer than necessary if I keep on speaking like this. Whatever I told you, consider it sufficient for now.

The untouchable class, which was considered only the servant of the society for a period of time, became empowered due to its service in the army. Furthermore, it succeeded in establishing its supremacy over other communities. There is no doubt in it that the Army service resulted in an unprecedented revolution in the Hindu social structure. The Marathas who had never even touched the Mahars and Chamars in the village, and who consider it their insult if a Mahar or a Chamar did not plead or greet them, the same Marathas bowed down and salute to the Havaldar Mahars or the Subedar Chamar. If they even said, 'hey you', no one had the courage to raise their eyes.

In other states of the country, the untouchable class could not get such rights. However, the untouchables of this state rise up in their status. Not only this, they made amazing progress in the field of education.

Ninety per cent of the people in the untouchable society were educated. Not only this, 50 per cent of the people were educated at a higher level. Significantly, the spread of education was not only among men but also among the women. Some women had attained such proficiency in education that they did commentary on Puranas (religious texts) in social gatherings. The credit for the progress in the field of education goes to the service they got in the army.

Why are the people who had made so much progress, are facing a downfall today? If seen on a superficial level, the condition of the untouchables in this area has become very pathetic. Such poverty, illiteracy and stupidity is not found among the untouchables of other states. This is a conundrum that how the untouchables of this state become like this? There could only be one answer to this question that this disaster happened because the British government has banned recruitment of untouchables in the army. There is no doubt in it that there is a great truth in this statement.

It is unjust to ban any person from a government job from political, moral or economic point of view. It would be said that barring untouchable community people from serving in the army is not only a sign of favouritism, but it is also a sign of treachery and treason.

Without the help of the untouchables, the British government could not have even entered this country. The historians give several reasons for how the British destroyed the Maratha Empire. Some say that the caste discrimination had increased to its pinnacle in the Maratha Empire. Some say that the Marathas were fighting among themselves. However, this is not the truth. In my opinion, if the Marathas had gone weak because of the increased caste discrimination and infighting, then were the British so capable? The truth is that when the British had established their supremacy over the country, that time Napoleon took England by surprise. The situation had become so serious that the British government was not in the position to provide financial assistance to the East India Company that was ruling over India. On the contrary, the British government had sought financial and military help from the East India Company to get rid of the clutches of the Napoleon.

Despite the British having such a weak position in India, how did they establish their supremacy over this country? The answer to this question cannot be that the Marathas were victim of their internal discord. In my opinion the real answer is something else. If the British had not raised this army, they would have never got this opportunity to rule over this country. Therefore, I appeal to the kind and just British Government to ask this question to themselves that who helped them in building the army at that time? They must see the old records of their army. Then will they come to know that only untouchables used to be recruited in the army at that time. There was no one else other than the untouchables in the army. This makes it clear that if the British were not backed by the power of the untouchables, they would never have become the rulers of this country.

Another example of how opportunistic the British are can be given. When World War I started in the year 1914, the British government remembered us. There is a great enthusiasm among our untouchable brothers to join the army. The government required one platoon (paltan) for recruitment in the army. However, men to the number equal to two platoons volunteered. The Government lifted ban on military recruitment imposed on the untouchables, which was enjoyed by all. The untouchables of this state were beginning to feel that good days were about to come again. Then the war ended, the platoon was again dismissed in the name of recession. What can be said about this dictatorial behaviour of the government?

Gentlemen, I am of the opinion that we are friendly towards the Government, is it not because this Government ignores us? We have been behaving like slaves by accepting whatever the government gives us, do what the government asks us to do, to do the way the government asks us to do. This is the main reason for our neglect by the government. We silently bear the injustice done to us, but our hand does not rise to retaliate. Even if the sky falls on us, we will bear it silently considering it as our destiny.

The sooner we give up this tendency, the better it will be in our interest. Therefore, I would like to tell you that we should keep trying for the reopening of the military recruitment as soon as possible.

But, I want to put a question before you. Will all our problems end automatically with the opening of recruitment in the army? In fact, many of our people think that once the army recruitment starts, then there is nothing left for us to do. I have a feeling that this is not true. It is certain that it is impossible to recruit all the people in the army. When the other class people were not at all ready to join the army, at that time there were ample opportunities for our people. However, today the situation is not like this. Now we will also get the same as what others will get. Now it is pointless to expect more than this. Now we have to think what more can be done for the progress of our community other than recruitment in the army.

There are very few people who are doing business from among the untouchable community. Chamars used to do business, but now they too are quitting their businesses. If you see in our community vast majority of people are without industry and business. There is a monopoly of a particular caste on any one business in this country. It would be meaningless if we say that you do that particular business. Those who want to do something should choose such a business, which is open to all castes. I see only two professions, in which one is to get a job and the other is agriculture.

I know this very well that the upper caste people do not like the preaching that untouchables should do jobs. They feel that the untouchables should work as the carpenters, blacksmiths, etc., and that they should not get into any decent job. I want to tell you this in clear words that this advice of theirs' is not beneficial for us. I believe that two things are very important for the reform of the untouchable society. First and foremost, it is very important to get rid of the bad thoughts that have taken over the mind.

Unless there is purity in thought, speech and conduct, the seed of awakening and progress cannot be sown in the untouchable society. Under the present circumstances, it is difficult for a new plant to thrive grow on our frigid minds. We need a job to be civilised. There is one more reason why the untouchables should have jobs. Whatever the government will think, it will be implemented accordingly. However, this should not be forgotten that whatever the government wants to do, will be done by its employees only. The government's opinion means opinion of its employees. It becomes very clear from this that if we want to get our interest from the government then we have to get a job. Secondly, the neglect that we are facing today will always remain the same.

If we have to work towards our welfare, then the untouchable community should get more and more government jobs. Our progress will be possible only from these jobs. The Muslim and Maratha community have completely understood the importance of this thing and their efforts are flowing in this direction. We should also wake up in time and try to get more and more employment. The Brahmins condemn it and say that the government job is useless. But there is no truth in their statement. The right to government jobs is in the hands of the Brahmins in this state. If this was not the case then the Brahmins of this state would have been cooks like those of the other states. If the supremacy of the Brahmins here were based on the Puranas then it would have collapsed long back. However, they have got government jobs. That's why their foundation is strong. The Brahmins have not given up their desire for the government jobs. On the contrary, they are very attached to it. Therefore, you people should not fall into the trap of false and unverified statements of the Brahmins.

Gentlemen, at this juncture I recall a sad fact. I have already related told you that at one time this area was replete with army Subedars. These people did many good things, but could not do one thing. If they had done that one work, it would have come in handy today. The main thing is that they did not educate their children. These people were not poor. They used to get a good pension during those days. Had the matter of education come to their mind at that time, they would have educated their children up to B.A., M.A. level. You can think of this too that what would have been the outcome? These educated children could have become Tehsildars, Collectors and Magistrates today and this untouchable society would not be in the pit. We would have flourished under their care. But for not being able to do this, today we are shrivelling under the sun to become thorns.

I firmly believe that our development is not possible making without making such efforts. Our development will be possible only by getting government jobs. Therefore, I am informing all of you to provide higher education to your children. The support that the society will get with one boy completing his BA will not be as much even if 1000 boys pass their fourth grade.

I would never say that primary education should be neglected. What I am saying is that the children getting higher education should be engaged in higher jobs as soon as possible. Therefore, it is very important to have a hostel for our boys in this locality. I intend to start a hostel at Panvel for the convenience of the students of Thane and Kolaba district. I wish that you all will cooperate financially in this work.

The second profession that I have suggested to you is agriculture. What I mean by suggesting this profession is may our untouchable society live their life independently. Of all the castes that exist in today's untouchable society, the status of the Mahars caste is that of the beggars. I have no hesitation in saying that this caste had developed the habit to go door-to-door every day to beg for stale food and subsist on it. Because of this there is no respect for this caste in the village. Their self-respect has been destroyed as a result of this practice. Say whatever, let him sit near the shoes, but give him loaves of bread... this has become the practice of this caste.

Due to this practice it is difficult for this caste to find the source of its progress independently. If they try to enter the temple today, they will even stop receiving the stale bread from the village. Therefore, sacrificing your humanity for the sake of stale bread is a matter of great shame. Is agriculture more difficult than begging for a piece of bread? It may be difficult for the untouchables to purchase agriculture land. However, the forest department has a lot of fallow land. If the untouchables demand that land, then it will not be difficult for them to get that land.

But how would all this will be possible? I believe that as long as we keep on receiving the bread to eat, our condition will remain the same. As long as the old path continues, no one will tread on the new path. Today we are far away from humanity because of the old path. How long is it going to continue like this? You must think about this.

Gentlemen, while bringing about new reforms the old lineage tradition is invoked. Is it okay to praise the old, even when it is too bad, and even if the new thing is very good? This means that if the ancestors have established a tradition in ignorance, then for how long their descendants will keep that wrong tradition alive? Always old is gold, sticking to this thinking will not bring in any new improvement.

Doesn't every parent want their children to be better off than them? How are the parents, who do not have this desire different from the pair of birds and animals? You should pay attention to what I'm saying, if not for yourself, at least for your children. The bread we are receiving today is enough, why bother for more? Why run after full bread leaving the half bread? You will ask such a question. But I want to warn you that if you do not follow the path that I am showing then you will not be able to get even today's stale bread.

It is not so that I have said this in front of you people only. I have expressed the same views wherever I had an opportunity to speak. The important thing is that all of you should do the work of awakening with enthusiasm. Ever since the army recruitment of the people of this state has stopped, the people of this state have subdued. All the activities have come to a standstill. This council is being organized after a long gap. The flame of awakening should never be extinguished. Some local leaders will be needed for this work. Any task seems difficult without guidance. All the pensioners of this place must pay attention to this, it is their duty. They should lead this great work of social upliftment, self upliftment. With this hope, I conclude my speech.

❑

# Mahad Satyagraha Council

This council was held on 25, 26, 27 December 1927 in Mahad. The pre-preparation for the council was done by Anant Vinayak Chitre. He was the main hero of the Mahad Satyagraha. The credit for the success of this council goes to Chitre. He reached Mahad fifteen days in advance for this programme.

Barring a few youths, all the upper caste people of Mahad were against this Satyagraha. They hatched such a conspiracy as the Council members could not get any kind of material and the work of the council gets messed up.

Under such circumstances, the organizers of the council resolved to make the council successful with the help of some youths of Kayastha caste. Shantaram Potnis, Keshavrao Deshpande, Vamanrao Patki, Kamlakar Tipnis etc. helped a lot. Of them we got generous cooperation from Vamanrao Patki. Had it not been for his help, the Parishad would not be able to get the material it needed for the programme. Every item had to be bought because of adverse situation in Mahad, due to which the council became expensive. Even in such a situation, Chitre and Patki did excellent organisation for the council, for which they deserve gratitude.

Subedar Ghatge from Pune, Thorat from Bhanagar and Bhangarkar Jamadar from came to Mahad on 24 December to support them. Subedar Ghatge was entrusted with the task of keeping the delegates present under discipline and making good arrangements of food for the huge assembly. On the other hand, the upper caste people of Mahad filed a suite against Dr. Ambedkar and four other untouchables to prevent untouchables from reaching Chavdar tank. Although, considering the importance of the meeting, the Collector and Superintendent of Police along with other officers had reached Mahad on 19th December itself.

Dr. Ambedkar left Bombay along with about 250 people on the Padmavati boat at 9 am on 24 December. He was accompanied by Shivtarkar, Dhondi Gaekwad, Kamble, Gangavane, Vanamali, Rajbhoj of Pune, Bhaurao Gaekwad of Nasik etc. Similarly, in the Social Service League, Sahastrabuddhe and the Pradhan brothers of Samata Sangha were among the upper caste householders. 'Brahman - Brahmanetar editor Devrao Naik, could not come due to bad health. The boat reached Hareshwar port at 5:30 pm. The public was already welcoming the satyagrahis with showering flowers.

Dr. Ambedkar had decided to go to Mahad via Dasgaon instead of Dharmatar. The people of Kolamand got the information about this. Hence they formed a committee to welcome the Satyagrahis coming from Bombay. Pandurang Mandlekar was the Chairman of the Welcoming Committee. The people of the village had made excellent arrangements. The Satyagrahis spent the night there comfortably. Next day after breakfast the Satyagrahis left for Dasgaon in the Ambe boat at 8. The boat reached Dasgaon at 12.30. Mahad was five miles away from Dasgaon. Around three thousand Satyagrahis were already waiting for Dr. Ambedkar to reach Mahad.

Police officers including Mr. Ferrante, Superintendent of Police of Kolaba district, Police Inspector, Faujdar etc. were already present. Superintendent of Police gave the letter from Collector Mr. Hood to Dr. Ambedkar after discussing with him. Thereafter Dr. Ambedkar and Sahasrabuddhe sat in Mr. Ferrante's motor and reached Mahad. Before leaving Dasgaon, Dr. Ambedkar informed all the Satyagrahis to come to Mahad with discipline and peace.

Sitaram Namdev Shivtarkar and Pradhan brothers reminded the satyagrahis present of Dr. Ambedkar words. The Satyagrahis left on foot in queues. The chants of "Har Har Mahadev", and "Mahad Satyagrah Ki Jai" continued. There were flags in the procession and some people were holding placards with motivational words. The volunteers of Bahishkrit Hitakarini Sabha (Untouchables Welfare Society) were marching with the band of the group. Singing the satyagraha songs, the Satyagrahi group of seven to eight thousand people reached the huge assembly hall, which was decorated with vines and arches.

The programme of the Parishad had to be changed as the Bombay satyagrahis could not reach Mahad on time. Therefore, the Council programme started at 4. First of all the children sang prayers to the God. Thereafter, C.N. Shivtarkar, secretary of the Satyagraha Committee, read the telegrams of Balwant Tilak and Dr. Purushottam Solanki and letters from other dignitaries (sympathy letters for the success of the Satyagraha Parishad). Later, amid thunderous applause, the chairman of the Satyagraha Committee, Dr. Ambedkar read out his speech—

Gentlemen,

You have come here today honouring the invitation of the Satyagraha Committee. As the Chairman of that Committee, I gratefully welcome you all.

Most of the friends present here would remember that on the 19th of March all of us went to the Chavadar Tank. The upper caste of Mahad did not oppose us at the Chavadar Tank then, but, they made an attack on us later. It is clear from all this that they oppose this work of ours. The result of this fight was that untouchables were sentenced to four months' imprisonment, and they are in jail today. If we had not been hindered on 19, 27 March, it would have been known that the upper caste acknowledge our right to draw water from the lake, and we would not have to organise our present campaign.

Unfortunately it is sad to state that nothing like this could happen. The upper caste of the Mahad are so wise that they fetch water from the Chavadar Lake themselves and they have also allowed the people from other religions to fill water. As a result, people from Muslim community also fill water from the Lake. Leave apart the humans, the upper caste people do not prevent even the birds and animals from drinking at the lake. This is not all, the animals reared by the untouchables are also allowed to drink water at the lake.

The Savarn Hindus are kind. They never resort to violence with anyone nor do they deceive anyone. The Savarn classes are not frugal and selfish. The proliferation of sages is the living testimony of their generosity. They consider charity as sacramental and grief as sin.

Not only this, it is their nature to regard other's suffering as their own. They not only treat the harmless cow with kindness, but also protect harmful creatures such as snakes. Therefore, it is their virtue that one soul dwells in all the creatures. Why is it so that such kind Savarn people forbids some human beings of their own religion to draw water from the same Chavadar Lake? Why do they get them arrested? These questions are bound to rise in anyone's mind.

What is the answer to this question? It is very essential that all should understand thoroughly the answer to this question.

Unless we do, I feel, you will not grasp the importance of today's meeting completely. There are four Varnas of Hindus as per the Shastras. However, as per customs and traditions, there are five varnas. (Brahmins, Kshatriyas, Vaishyas, Shudras and Atishudras). It is the first of the governing rules of the Hindu religion. The second is the unequal ranks of the castes. They are ordered in a descending series of each meaner than the one before.

Categories have been fixed according to the rules in the caste system. Not only this, then who is of what status? That's why the limit to the Varnas has been fixed. In Hindu religion, the limits of beti bandi, roti bandi, lota bandi and uphar bandi (exchanges of daughter, bread, water and gifts) have been set, this is the common thinking. But, this thinking is incomplete. These four types of bonds or behaviours have a limit. But, they have been determined to mark the status of people of unequal status, that is, this borderline of non-cohabitation manifests inequality.

Just as he who wears crown on head is called a king, similarly he who wields the bow and arrows in his hand is called a Kshatriya. In the similar fashion, the class which is free of the aforementioned prohibitions is considered superior. On the contrary, to which they all apply is reckoned the lowest in rank. The strenuous efforts made to preserve this tetragon so that equality cannot establish within the inequality as determined by religion.

The Savarn people of the Mahad don't want the untouchables to drink water of the Chavadar Lake. The reason for this is not that touched by the untouchables the water will become profane or evaporate and vanish. The only reason for preventing the untouchables from drinking it is that they do not wish to acknowledge that they are equal to us by allowing the castes that have been declared inferior by the Shastras to draw water from the Lake.

Gentlemen! We have started this dispute. What is the meaning of this dispute? You might know it. The Satyagraha Committee has invited you to Mahad. You should never understand that you have only been invited here to drink the tasty water of the Chavadar Lake of Mahad.

It is not that drinking the water of the Chavadar Lake will make us immortal. We have not drunk the water of the Chavadar Lake till date. So have we died? We don't have to go to the Chavadar Lake merely to drink its water. We are going to the lake to assert that we too are human beings like others. Therefore, it is clear that this meeting has been called to set up the norm of equality.

If we look at it from this perspective then we will know that this meeting is very important. I believe that no one would have a doubt in this regard. It is an unprecedented day today. I believe that no example parallel to it can be found in the history of India.

Some of our brothers might feel that we are untouchables and, therefore, it is enough if we are set free from the prohibitions of inter-drinking and social intercourse. This is not the case. And, we have no concern with the system. If it is also there then we have no objection to it. In my opinion this thinking is absolutely wrong. People would say that the idea of ending untouchability by keeping the Varnashrama system intact is unrealistic. The way external efforts are necessary for the welfare of the humans, aspiration is also needed in a similar way. There is always a doubt that whether efforts are possible without aspiration. Hence, if a great effort is to be made, a great aspiration must be nursed. Without a strong will, there remains a doubt whether effort will be possible in the hands of a man or not. If a big work is to be done, it has to be done accordingly. You have to have a very strong desire. There is no reason to be ashamed and afraid of whether a wish will come true or not. We should be ashamed of having petty desires.

When untouchability is removed, we will be holier than the Atishudras, but making Shudras from Atishudras does not mean the complete abolition of untouchability. Abolition of untouchability is a proposal — If I could finish this task merely with a petty wish of ending the caste system, that is, untouchability would have ended, then I would not have asked you to abolish the caste system. You know that to kill a snake, nothing will happen by hitting its tail, rather we will have to crush its head. To destroy a troublemaker, one must strike at the core. Where does the death of a wicked person occur? Only after identifying it, you have to attack that spot. Duryodhana was killed when Bhima hit his thigh with a mace. If the mace had hit his head, he would not have died. The cause of Duryodhana's death was in the thigh and not in the head.

It is noteworty in this regard that untouchability cannot be completely destroyed by mere imposition of ban and philosophising. As a result of these two, maximum that can happen is the untouchability may end outside the house but it will be remain as it is. In order to abolish untouchability inside as well as outside the house, we will have to end the betibandi. Anyone will agree that this is the only way to establish equality. The stems will die on their own if the main stem (root) is destroyed. All these problems of rotibandi, lotabandi and giftbandi have arisen because of betibandi only. When betibandi ends, there will be no need to solve other problems. They will automatically end. From my point of view, breaking the dam of betibandi is the right act to remove untouchability and only this will establish true equality. If we want to destroy untouchability, then we have to accept that the root cause of untouchability is betibandi. Today, if our attack is on lotabandi, then our ultimate target should be on betibandi. Without this there will be no complete upliftment of untouchability. Who can do this work? There is no need to tell that the Brahmin class will not do this work. Complete eradication of untouchability will not be possible.

As long as the caste system lasts, the Brahmin class will have its supremacy. No one will voluntarily forgo the power he wields in his hands. The Brahmin class has exercised their sovereignty over all other classes for centuries. It is not likely that they will be willing to forgo it and treat the rest as equals. The Brahmins do not have the same patriotism as of the Samurais of Japan. It is useless to hope that they will sacrifice their privileges as the Samurai class did, for the sake of national unity based on a new equality. The non-Brahmin class, i.e. the Marathas and other similar castes, are a class between the privileged and those without any rights or the unprivileged.

A privileged class, at the cost of a little self-sacrifice, can show some generosity. However, a class without any privileges has ideals and aspirations to bring a social revolution. Therefore, it has the quality of theoreticism rather than of selfishness. The Brahmin class that falls between the two, lacks the generosity and principles. This is why this class, instead of directly facing the Brahmins is more conscious about maintaining its privilege over the untouchables.

This is a disabled class from the point of view of social revolution. If we expect things from this class, it will prove futile. We have to complete the task of removing untouchability and establishing equality that we have undertaken on ourselves. This work is not possible by the hands of anyone else other than you. We must consider that we are born to carry out this task and set to work in earnest. This is the meaning of our lives. We should accept the virtue that we are receiving.

This work also is of enlightenment. This work will remove the obstacles coming in the way of our progress. We all must realise that untouchability has added filth to our food. It is known to all that, at one time, we were abundant in the army, we held monopoly in the service of the army. That's why we didn't need to worry about our livelihood. Today other people in equal number to us are seen on the job in the army, police, court, tribunal, but not a single person from among us is on the job in these departments today.

It is not so because the law debars us from these jobs. Everything is permissible as far as the law is concerned. But because the Hindus consider us untouchables and look down upon us, the government also ignores us. And this is the reason we are being kept out of Government jobs. We cannot do any work with our head held high. Nor can we take up any decent trade for lack of money. It is also true to some extent that the people are not ready to buy goods from us due to untouchability. This the main obstacle if we undertake any business.

In all, untouchability is not a simple matter. It is the mother of all our poverty and lowliness, therefore today we in this dire crisis. If we want to raise ourselves out of this inferiority complex, we must undertake this task in our own hands. We cannot succeed without doing this. It is a task not for our benefit alone but it is also for the benefit of the nation.

No good can happen to the Hindu society without eradication of the untouchability in this Chaturvarna (four-castes) system. Social morality is a very important tool in the means that society uses to remove mutual discord. This fact has to be accepted. Things which are harmful to the unity of the society are considered worthy whereas things which bind the society together are despised. Such a society has to accept defeat in its internal strife. On the contrary, the morality of the society is such that where social unity is praised and the reasons which lead to the disintegration of the society, those reasons are condemned. Then in such a society, even if there is discord in life, one does not remain without fame.

The same principle applies to the Hindu social system. The four-varna system is a public diversion system, whereas the single-varna system is a public collection system. If we keep praising the destructive system even after seeing it with naked eyes and Hindu society have to suffer at every step, then why be surprised with it? If this picture has to be changed, then the four-tone system has to be abolished and a one-tone system has to be established.

Even this will not be enough to complete this task. The inequality inherent in the four-caste system must also be up rooted. Many people mock at the principles of equality. Naturally, no two men are equal. Some are physically strong, whereas others are weak. Some have a sharp intellect and some have a dull one.

The saying of egalitarian people that they should be considered equal even if they are born unequal is not correct. In fact, it has to be said that these devils have not understood the meaning of equality.

The attainment of rights should not be based on one's birth or property, rather it should be on the basis of one's merits. If this is what equality means, then the person who is virtueless, dirty and wrong, and the person who is virtuous, clean and right - should be treated equally.

How can such an expectation be made? Such counter-question is asked. While explaining the equality, it is said that persons similar in quality should be treated equally.

Although after the qualities have been developed in a person, before coming to the position of power, why should they be so unequal? Equal treatment is appropriate. According to Sociology, the social system plays an important role in the complete development of the qualities of an individual. If a slave is always treated unequally, he will have no other quality than slavery. This slave will not be eligible for any other qualification and authority. Similarly, if a holy person despises a profane person and mutual reconciliation stops, then the desire to become holy will never arise in the profane person. Morality can never start in an immoral person if persons or the society with moral values does not shelter him.

The examples given above certainly prove that, although an equal treatment may not generate good qualities of one person in another in another, yet it is true that the natural qualities does not develop without the treatment of equality. Similarly, without the behavior of equality, the qualities of a person are not appreciated.

On the one hand, the inequality in Hindu society stunts the progress of individuals and on the other hand, the same inequality prevents the use for the society the qualities and powers accumulated in an individual. The four-caste system further weakens the already divided Hindu society.

If the Hindu society is to be strengthened, then we must uproot the four-caste system and untouchability, and set the Hindu society on the foundations of the two principles – equality and one-caste system. The abolition of untouchability will invigorate the Hindu society. Therefore, I say that our task is for the benefit of the nation as it is in our own interest.

We have commenced this task to bring about a social revolution. No one should suppose that it is a diversion to quieten the minds with sweet words. This task of ours is based on the feeling. This same feeling is working as the power behind our task. This is the reason that it is not possible for anyone to stop the momentum of this task. It is my wish that that the social revolution that is being unfolded here today should be completed quickly.

We wish to say to our opponents that please do not oppose us. Put aside the orthodox scriptures and respect the justice. We assure you that we shall carry out our programme peacefully.

## Proposals presented by Babasaheb Ambedkar in the Mahad Council –

Social injustice, religious slander, political decadence and economic slavery cause the downfall of the nation. I have a clear opinion that the living example of this is the Hindu culture in this area. The main reason for the plight of the Hindu society is that what are the birthrights? Bahujan Samaj has not realized its need and awareness nor has curbed the progress of selfish elements. It is the supreme duty of every citizen of the society to know their birthright, exercise it and not allow it to be violated in mutual dealings. What are the birthrights of Hindu society? It should always be before the eyes of every Hindu. Therefore, in this meeting, the following declaration is being issued for the information of all —

## First Proposal

1. All humans are equal by birth; and shall remain equal till death. They may vary in status only in the public utility. Yet, their equal status must be maintained. There should be no obstacle in the practice of the principle of equality and no such action should be taken. Such is the opinion of the meeting.

2. May the above mentioned birth rights of human remain intact, this should be the ultimate goal of the polity and social system. Therefore, the meeting strongly condemns the unequal social structure of the Hindu society and the ancient and modern words that support it.

3. Akhil Praja (the entire populace) is the originator of all forms of authority and power. Special rights of any individual, community or class, shall not be valid if the Bahujan (majority) has not given such rights, whether political or religious. Similarly, in the context of social system, the meeting is not ready to accept the evidence of scriptures like Shruti, Smriti, Purana etc.

4. Any person is free to act according to his birthright. Any limit imposed upon this freedom must be only to the extent necessary to permit other persons to enjoy their birthrights. Such limits must be laid down by law. These limits should

be governed by the rules made by the people. They cannot be set on the grounds of the religion/scriptures or on any other basis. The assembly forbids the unequal system prescribed in caste or caste like Ashtadhikar.

5. Things that are dangerous to the society should be forbiden by the law. No one else should be able to refuse unless prohibited by law. No one can deny the use of public roads, public places, public wells, ponds and temples. This assembly understands that if anyone does this, then these people are enemies of orderly society and justice.

6. The law is not in the nature of bounds laid by any particular class. How is the law? The right to decide it shall rest with entire public or their representatives. Whether such a law is protective or punitive, shall apply to all equally. Equality being the basis of social formation, caste should not become a hindrance in respect, rights and business. The distinction should be on the basis of merits of any person and not on the basis of his birth. Therefore, the assembly strongly condemns the caste-based discrimination and inequality.

## Second Proposal

Keeping in mind the words of Manusmriti, those who insult the people from Shudra caste, stop their progress, destroy their self-confidence and create social, political and economic slavery, compare the elements of the Declaration of the Birthright of Hindus from the above-mentioned texts (Manusmriti), are not fit to bear the holy name of any scripture. It is the opinion of this assembly and in order to express its opinion, it burns this anti-people book that destroys humanity.

## Third Proposal

All the followers of Hindu religion should be considered as one caste, the entire Hindu society should be identified by this noun

'Hindu'. There should be a legal ban on addressing by caste-related nouns of Brahmins, Kshatriyas, Vaishyas, Shudra etc. Such is the opinion of this assembly. There is no objection to the naming on the basis of occupation like tailor, goldsmith, gardener etc. and on the basis of province like Maratha, Kokanastha, Deshastha etc.

## Fourth Proposition

This Council opines that –

The Dharmadhikari (pujari) should be the follower of the public and appointed by the public.

Every Hindu should have the right to accept and acquire the eligibility for the position of the Dharmadhikari (priest).

The Dharmadhikari should be issued a certificate after giving him examination. Until such certificate has been obtained, one shall be legally prohibited from being called Dharmadhikari and carrying out any legal work.

Such a scheme should be done by Village Dharmadhikari, Tehsil Dharmadhikari and province Dharmadhikari.

The above appointed religious functionaries should not be entitled to receive any dakshina, labour or reward for performing religious rituals. Like the officials of other departments, the junior and senior officers of this department should also be treated as the government employees and they should also be paid the appropriate salary by the government.

❑

# Ramabai's Self Sacrifice

'Marathas attacked Saheb (Ambedkar) in Raigad fort, he is in the hospital', hearing this fake news Ramabai started to cry. Women tried to calm her down. Everyone told Babasaheb, "Please go home, so that Ramabai may feel good."

Babasaheb said angrily that "all women are like this only. If we keep caring for their wishes and aspirations, we would not be able to do any good. I have to take the train in the night to Kolhapur for a case, and now I have to prepare for the case. You all should go."

Babasaheb spoke to Ramabai after returning from Kolhapur. He went to his office after he spoke to her. Sahasrabuddhe said to Babasaheb Ambedkar in the office that, "Sir, you are very careless towards your wife, it is not good." Babasaheb got very serious on this and said, "You all are accusing me, but I too love my wife, children and my library with all my heart. My way of showing love is not like that of yours. That's why I seem cruel to you. However, this is totally wrong. In fact it is because of the self-sacrifice of my wife that I have achieved this position today.

# Why Satyagraha?

Today we are going to enter the temple. But this is not at all possible that all your questions will be solved after entering the temple. The nature of your questions is broad. Their nature is political, social, religious, economic and educational. But today's Kalaram Temple Entry Satyagraha is a call to the mindset of the upper class Hindus. For hundreds of years the upper caste Hindus has kept us away from the humanity. These upper caste Hindus are not ready to give us the rights of humanity. This question is going to be evident with the temple entry Satyagraha. The upper caste Hindus have considered us inferior even to the cats and dogs. If still Hindus are ready to remunerate the humanity to humans like us or not? We are about to get the answer to this question from this Satyagraha. This Satyagraha is to change the core of the hearts of Hindus. Through this Satyagraha, an attempt is being made to bring about a change in the hearts of upper caste Hindus. However, will it be successful or not? It all depends on the mindset of the Hindus.

It is not at all like that all our questions will be instantly resolved as soon as we get entry in the Ram temple. It is not that that after entering the temple all our problems will be solved and we will be transformed. We are testing the minds of the upper caste Hindus. Humans should be treated like human beings, humans should get the rights of humanity and the humanity should be established. It is being tested that in this new age, is the Hindu mind ready to accept this higher inspiration or not? We have decided to hold this Satyagraha to achieve this. Will the upper caste Hindus think about it or not? This is the main question that what are they going to do? We know that there is a stone idol in the temple. Seeing the idol and worshiping it would not solve our problems. Millions of people have visited this temple till date and have had the darshan of the Goddess. However, we know that their fundamental questions were not solved by the darshan. However, today's Satyagraha is to bring about change in the hearts of the Hindus. We are going to take the step of Satyagraha with a special motive today.

❑

# Should There Be Satyagraha?

Should Satyagraha be held at Kalaram Temple in Nashik on Ram Navami? It is very kind of you to have asked me my views on this subject. However, now I do not feel any emotion while telling that it is not appropriate to hold the Satyagraha there. The movement to enter the temple should not merely be suspended but stopped altogether. This may appear surprising that the one who had suggested to carry out the Satyagraha is now advising to cease the movement. I am also having a feeling of dread in declaring this change. I launch the movement of entry into the temple. The purpose of this movement was that the depressed classes should gain the entry in the temple and start to worship the idol so that they may achieve salvation. It was not at all appropriate to live life with such kind of thinking. I have never thought it in this manner. I never had the opinion nor will I ever think in this way that by gaining entry in the temple, the untouchables would get equal respect in the Hindu society. The purpose of this movement was to make the untouchables aware of their human rights and to awake the consciousness in them so that they can fight against their adversaries to win their human rights. I believe I have achieved that purpose. This Satyagraha should culminate in the spread of education and struggle for political rights to the untouchables of Maharashtra and India. If the untouchable community is enriched by education and becomes influential and powerful by political rights, it will continue to be an outstanding component of the Hindu society. However, to achieve this, necessary changes should take place in the Hindu society, religion and the religious scriptures. For this, the untouchables will have to keep on fighting to motivate the upper caste Hindus to do this work. There should be necessary changes in the religion and religious scriptures. For this, the untouchables will have to keep on fighting to inspire the upper caste Hindus to do this work.

❑

# Stone in the Bag

Workers like Bhaurao Gaikwad, Rankhambe, Dani etc. were jailed without any reason. Similarly, I regret to hear that the aged mother of Tulsiramji Kale and the mother of Amritrao Rankhambe have been taken prisoner. However, I also felt blessed. I am very proud of my untouchable brothers of the Nashik district. In the last three to four years the way the untouchables have worked with self-reliance and organizational skill in adverse and difficult conditions is unprecedented. The enthusiasm and courage with which my sisters have presented their work is outstanding. No help is extended from anyone nor is there any sympathy from anyone. On the contrary, everyone is angry for one or the other reason and has become rivals. In such circumstances, the depressed classes with the help of the untouchables and for the untouchables endeavoured with great enthusiasm for three to four years got together in a huge number to organize the Nashik Satyagraha movement. There is no exaggeration in saying that this incident is a matter of pride for all the Dalits not only in India but in the entire world. But, the Hindu society that has been made foolish, intolerant and ungrateful by the Brahmin religion, what would they be concern with all this? Through this Satyagraha movement, at least, the untouchable women demanded for their equality along with the untouchable Hindus. They sought the bread of equality and love from their Hindu brothers. But, the Brahminical Hindus pelted stones at the untouchables.

❑

# Round Table Conference

The thought that I will not be able to meet you all for the next five-six months, aches my heart. I have done a lot in the past two years. I would not be able to do anything single handed had thousands of gentlemen not helped me. My friend Dr. Solanki has helped me a lot in the work done by me in the Bar Council. The governor called me in the year 1926 and asked, "If Dr. Solanki is elected to the Bombay Law Council as the representative of the untouchables, then will you and he join the Council or not?" To this I had replied, "Since Dr. Solanki is well educated, therefore both of us will be compatible to each other. I am little outspoken and a bit short tempered. When I was in the Council I might have exhibited the same attitude towards Dr. Solanki at time too. However, he helped me without keeping any grudge in his heart. Therefore, the credit for all the works of the Council goes to Solanki only.

The Samata Sangha has helped me a lot in things outside the Council. Mr. Devrao Naik has helped me till date, and therefore

I consider him my right hand. I believe that even if I stay abroad for five–six months, we understood each other by being together. Hence in my absence, Mr. Naik will take this work further. My other friends from Samata Sangh Mr. Pradhan, Kadrekar, Kavadi etc. have also helped a lot. Similarly, Shri Shankarrao Parasha had immensely helped in money matters. There is no other pillar of support like Shri Shankarrao. Money is needed in public work. When I started boarding at Solapur, I had only Rs. 500/- with me. I borrowed Rs. 1000/- from a Jewish friend by writing a promissory note and started a boarding at Solapur. Shri Shankarrao had helped a lot in this. He helped with finance to buy (a press with Rs. 1800/-). a lot of people are cooperative partners in many works.

Several of my friends and colleagues feel that I am not poetic by nature. Even I think so. My nature and attitude may not be poetic, but isn't my life becoming a unique and profound poem? An untouchable and Mahar boy from India will come forward to participate in the Round Table Conference and will actively participate in the future of the nation building. Has anyone ever thought of this? Even the flight of imagination gets handicapped, we don't even analyse that. So, is this incident not filled with poem and miracle? This is called incredibly beautiful poetry or in other words romance. What could be more unprecedented for them than my life?

It is not possible for others, but when I went to New York for higher education because of the generosity of the King of Baroda, my life began with the aim to pursue my interests through study. However, in such a short span of time, being one with the joys and sorrows of my voiceless dalit society, my life would become public and significant. Even I didn't ever imagine it myself. My people love me a lot. Am I worthy of this? It can be considered the game of future. Although it is that my insignificant and unpoetic life has got a meaning. The nature has entrusted me this work considering it as a means of salvation for my people. The satisfaction that comes from this realization is rare. This opportunity comes to a very few people.

I accept this fund and certificate of honour given by you. However, I am not using this money for my personal work at all. It will be used only for the poor people. I have agreed to deposit some amount on behalf of Bombay State to meet the expenses of the Central Organization of All India Dalit Congress. Therefore, I am depositing some part of this amount with Dr. Solanki. He should use this fund for the Dalit Congress. The remaining fund will be used for some other purposes. I wish that our fortnightly "Bahishkrit Bharat" that has been suspended, might start again. Articles will be published in this newspaper after reviewing the current situation. I have decided to rename the fortnightly. The reason being, that several people don't subscribe our paper because of its name. What is your opinion? Everyone should understand this. Earlier, this objective of ours was not achievable. Therefore, I decided to change the name. The name of the fortnightly will be 'Janata' and Mr. Devrao Naik will be its editor. Therefore you are kindly requested to associate members/readers with the newsletter. Part of the fund will be given to the boarding for help. This way the fund will be utilised.

The British Government will be bearing the expenses of my visit abroad for the Round Table Conference. Then why this fund? But I didn't expect any help from you even when I needed it. Today I do not need your help for my personal expenses. When I need, I will definitely ask you people. The Untouchable class will definitely get benefited by my going to the Round Table Conference. But the people have boycotted this Conference. I want to ask them that at a time when two groups of people are in confrontation, what's wrong in speaking the language of agreement? Today there is an internal struggle going on between the government and the Congress. Congress movement is harming the government. Both the parties are being adamant on their respective stand. In this situation settlement is possible by some mediation at the Round Table Conference. It is said by some that no outcome is expected from this Conference. But I differ. Those who think that this Conference will fail are asked how and why the conference will fail?

At present Hindus, Muslims, Untouchables all want Swarajya. Earlier, Akhil Dalit Congress also had adopted a similar proposal in Nagpur. Everyone is unanimous. The only difference is the method as to how Swarajya should be given? How would minorities secure the social, religious and political equality? Wanted such a Swarajya where all the Hindus should be independent. But the controversy is that should the power that comes with Swaraj be properly distributed in the entire society or should it be in the hands of a special class! If the progressive class and the majority demonstrate generosity of mind for the solution of problems of Dalit society, backward class and minority class then the end of the conflict is not impossible.

They will ask for what they want. But at the same time if such proposal which demands Swarajya to this country comes, I will support it. Like Congress, we also feel that this country should reach the pinnacle of greatness by progressing in every way. In the end, after the Round Table Conference is over, I want to do one more thing and that is—to awaken public opinion. This is a very important task. Congress movement is taking place in countries like America, Germany etc. We have to convey our (Dalits') sufferings to others as well. I will meet prominent leaders and put my grief before them. Not only this, if possible I would put questions of untouchables in front of the League of Nations. At present police and army jobs are closed for untouchables. I will try my best to get this ban uplifted. Finally, I have only one request for everyone to act in unison. There are several factions among us. In last couple of years, I have seen a strange development. Everyone calls himself a leader. This is very bad. Such things should stop in future, this is my request.

There are so many obstacles before us and there is a mountain of work before us, for which no district or province can do anything. Rather all Dalit brothers will have to work shoulder to shoulder, keeping aside their mutual differences. In this lies the interest of all of us. In my absence the awareness created in the society by working as per the views of Dr. Solanki and Shri. Naik, I hand over responsibility of furthering this awareness to you. The difference between untouchables and Muslim minority society and the majority society of Hindu Congress etc. exists even today. Five different minority societies had prepared a draft together. Ignoring their attempts to compromise and rather taking this as a warning given to us, the representatives of the majority class like the Congress and the Hindu Mahasabha opposed it, leading to further deepening of differences.

It is incomprehensible, but now the intensity of the opposition by Gandhiji (with regard to the demands made by me for untouchables) has subsided. It seems that if we take firm steps, Gandhiji will not show a belligerent face to fulfill his resolve to oppose the demands of untouchables till he goes to Bombay. Last night Gandhiji and I met again. The credit for this meeting goes to the Diwan of Mysore, Sir Mirza Ismail. Fair-minded people feel that the treatment meted out by Gandhiji towards me was unfair. Blind devotees of Mahatma, who find no fault in Gandhiji's behaviour feel that once the untouchables get the right of self-determination, the majority will no longer be in their hands. This fear of theirs is selfish. Barring the Hindu representatives, Gandhiji's policy towards me is not fair.

Gandhiji asked me, "Would you be ready to make some changes in the demands that you have put forward for the protection of the Untouchables?" Then I said, "I and fellow members and my friends and leaders of untouchable society are always ready for any worthy change." Hearing this, he put his new plan before me. According to this scheme, if an untouchable candidate standing in the election from the joint constituency is not elected, he should file a complaint in the court and prove that - I and the candidate who is elected against me, we both have the same abilities. I did not come of my own free will because I am an untouchable, while he came of his own free will. On telling this to the court and upon the court giving its decision wherein the membership of that Hindu representative will be considered cancelled and untouchable candidate will be appointed.

This plan was so impractical that only Gandhiji had the courage to point it out. I laughed for a moment. I thought, perhaps it was Gandhiji's humour. But there were no expressions of laughter and humour on his face. He asked me seriously, “How do you like this plan of mine?” I said calmly, “Not at all right.” He asked, “Why?” On this I said “This plan of yours is absolutely impractical.” That was how our meeting ended. I came back after taking leave from Gandhiji. But in this unsuccessful meeting, I saw a ray of hope towards Gandhiji - I give, so the untouchable society shall be grateful and satisfied. It is okay if he dies, but nothing is going to be given to him. Untouchables, in addition to general voting rights, will not get any special facility like reserved seat etc. Gandhiji should not have, at least, taken a pledge to fast unto death.

The second topic for discussion which came before us was that— ‘according to which system between Hindu representative and the government should there be political progress of India?’ It was a struggle. At present, the government is considering giving only provincial autonomy. The Central government is not ready to make India independent. But because of this controversy, what is the ultimate limit of this responsible self-government and what is the definitive form of the Protective bond? This was a major question of importance, as it was lying on the sidelines. We, the minorities, have accepted the policy that we also want self-government (provincial and central) of responsibility.

The King invited all the delegates on tea in the afternoon of 5th November. All Hindu princely states including Gandhiji and

European delegates were present. The Emperor had pre-selected ten people to say something as a courtesy, and I was one of them. When it was my turn to talk to the king, I remembered my childhood. I felt like standing in front of Guruji on my first day in school. What to say to the Maharaja? What to tell? I could not understand. Then, dispelling my worries, the King asked me what is the situation of untouchability in India? I gave information about untouchables in a few words. As I apprised him, it turned out that Raja Saheb was already aware of many things. He expressed his regret over the plight of the excluded class. Upon telling about the fact, his lips and feet were trembling. What was the extent of my education and what did my father do? He discussed with affinity.

Day before yesterday I had a long talk with the chief Pradhan. We had a discussion on what are the things beneficial for the untouchable society? On the last 10$^{th}$, I had given a speech in an organization called 'Institute of International Affairs'. This event was organized with the objective that the representatives of the minority society should get an opportunity to present their views before the British people. In my speech, I mentioned the need for the demands of untouchables and discussed how important it is today. Sir Mohammad Shafi presented the case of Muslims. Sardar Ujjwal Singh put the point of Sikhs. Sir Herbert Carr supported the demands of the European Society. This programme was very successful. Gandhiji and other representatives on behalf of Congress and Bahujan Hindu Samaj presented their aspect to the British people and it was very important to present the other aspect as well.

What is Gandhiji's aptitude and policy on the question of a particular caste? It is very clearly evident from his speech given by him in the Constitution Committee and Federal Structure Committee. What should be the composition of the Federal Legislature? we were discussing this question that in that proof and what basis will the members be selected? At that time

Gandhiji's policy on the question of caste (particular) became clear. As a representative of the Congress, I am ready to give independent representation to the Muslim and Sikh communities only. The Untouchables and other minority communities should be satisfied only on the assurance of the voting system. They will not get any other facility. Such an explanation was given by Gandhiji in his speech. How is his policy wrong? I didn't get a chance to explain because Gandhi's speech took place after mine? So the question remained as it is.

The meeting of the minority sub-committee was to be held on 26th September. This day was round the corner. One day Mr. Devdas Gandhi (Gandhiji's son) came over and said to me, "My father wants to see you." I said, "Okay."

I met Gandhiji at Sarojini Naidu's residence as per the pre-arranged time and suggestion. As usual he said to me, "You tell me, what do you want?"

"What do we want? this has already been clearly stated. The same question must be asked again and again and answered again and again, this is not particularly satisfactory and promising." Yet what I ask on behalf of the untouchables and why do I ask? If I again tell Gandhiji, who may not have the correct idea (probably), then there is no harm if he answers again. Considering this, I stated the demands in detail and with evidence. The meeting lasted for three hours from 8:00 PM to 11:00 PM. Gandhiji was spinning yarn and was listening to me attentively. He asked me questions from time to time. He didn't let even a trace of his thoughts be revealed to me. In fact, Gandhiji should have had a frank discussion with me. Letting the views of the opposition out but not letting your views unveil is called Chanakya policy. But in this context it was irrelevant and unnecessary.

If I had that in my mind, I too could have played this trick. But what was it going to achieve? As per the directives of the Congress, it was necessary for Gandhiji to oppose my demands. Even if it was considered necessary, then also it could have been done after discussing with an open mind and trust. I would have not opposed it. I would have understood his protest sympathetically. But sadly, the openness I showed to Gandhiji was not able to do that. Gandhiji did not speak openly after listening to me completely. I would have been forced to do so. However, Sarojini Naidu signalled me to not to say anything. She said, "Everything will be as per your wish, just be patient."

I also gave up the idea of asking Gandhiji. It was very late. Naidu was hungry. It was eleven o'clock. I bid farewell to Gandhiji and went out. Gandhiji had met Jinnah before he met me. I came to know later about the settlement Gandhiji and Jinnah had for the rights of Muslims.

The meeting of the committee appointed to consider the minority question began under the chairmanship of Ramsey MacDonald. As per the strategy of Gandhiji with the Muslim representatives, today's meeting should have been postponed and more time should be given on the questions of the minorities for mutual agreement. Gandhiji had made a proposal to this effect. Aga Khan supported his proposal. In fact, even before this proposal came, he had taken the consent of the Muslim and Sikh representatives and took them into confidence. He should have treated us too in the same way. I could not have opposed the proposal for a long time. He considered the questions of minorities before the committee, but only after first discussing it with the Muslim and Sikh representatives. However, what does not discussing with Hindu representatives and other representatives indicate? 'Call me and listen to my demands for three hours but don't say anything on your part and bring a motion to adjourn the meeting and take my objections and say that Dr. Ambedkar opposes.' Gandhiji gave freedom to his followers and devotees to spread propaganda against me and blamed me for my reaction. I was accused of rashness and arrogance, is this Gandhi's policy?

However, no matter how many allegations are there, still this policy of Gandhi has to be answered. I stood up to oppose Gandhiji's proposal (Gandhiji categorically refused to give free electorates and reserved seats to the untouchables) and I said that there is nothing left to talk to him on behalf of the untouchables. Therefore, the committee should consider our demands and should dispense justice to us. Everyone was surprised to see my protest. MacDonald, the chairman and the chief of the committee, looked at Gandhiji and asked him to reply. However, instead of answering my objection, he said, "I am bound by the decisions of the Congress. What has the Congress expressed about the untouchables and what had they decided to do for them?" After such a detailed speech, no solution was found. Finally, Gandhiji said that the Congress was ready to give representation only to the Muslim and the Sikh communities. The Congress is unwilling to give caste-specific facilities like separate electorates or reserved seats to the untouchables. If the representatives of the Muslim minority community accept your demands, then the authority to grant recognition on behalf of the Congress is in my hands. After this assurance given by the Gandhiji, there was no reason for me to oppose the postponement of the motion. Hence, I withdrew my protest.

After this nothing special has happened. Gandhiji met the Muslim representatives a couple of times. He did not discuss anything with other minority communities. But, one day out of nowhere he suddenly invited me, the representatives of the Christian and Anglo-Indian community. Subsequently, we met him. He again asked, "What do you want?" I also read along with everyone, the mountain of demands of the untouchables. This time Pandit Madan Mohan Malaviya was also present there. After listening to us, Gandhiji said angrily, "How will your demands be fulfilled? I am unable to understand that.'' We refused to withdraw our demands regardless of malice and greed. We bid him farewell and as we were about to leave, he said, "Now I will tell the chief representative that our differences are not going to end and efforts for reconciliation have failed. Now I do not need more time for adjournment." But, there was no reason to be intimidated by Gandhiji's threat. We decided that now we will put our points directly before the committee.

When the committee meeting resumed, Gandhi surprised them by moving an adjournment motion himself. Gandhiji says something and does something else. It cannot be anticipated accurately. However, this time I did not oppose his proposal. This time a three-tier committee was formed to deal with caste-specific questions, and Gandhiji was chosen as the Chairman of this committee. Gandhiji put forth three important questions.

1. Which society or caste needs representation in the system?
2. Whether this representation will come from the joint or free election system?
3. How many seats will be given to the community that will come to give the free representation?

According to this plan, Gandhiji asked representatives of untouchables, Muslims, Sikhs, Hindus, Christians, Anglo-Indians and Europeans to express their views. All of us public views put forth our views. Later, Gandhiji took a different stand and said, "It is all impossible." He did not even attempt to solve the question. The question put forth by the minorities was difficult, but not impossible. After this, meetings were held twice under the Chairmanship of Gandhiji. However, due to his attitude no one participated enthusiastically in the discussion.

Eventually this period also ended. We could not reach an agreement. Tomorrow again the same thing will have to be presented before the minority committee and MacDonald. Sarojini Naidu suggested a strategy to avert this embarrassing situation, "We all should be ready to hand over the Punjab Question to the mediation committee. Other questions are on the way to be resolved. By declaring this, the embarrassing situation must be avoided." However, a standoff arose between the Sikhs and the Muslims. They said, we will decide after deliberation. It was 8 o'clock in the evening amidst all these discussions. Therefore, everyone was expected to assemble after three hours, at 11 O'clock, and Muslims-Sikhs have to give their decision according to the information of Sarojini Naidu.

We all gathered again at 11 o'clock. I had given an information regarding Punjab. Keeping in mind the problem of untouchables, the tribunal which will be formed to give decision on the question of Punjab, should give the clear information about decision in context of Hindus, Muslims and Sikhs. Otherwise I will have to oppose the decision of the tribunal. But, other public representatives did not allow such a time to come. On the question of Punjab, the original plan of Naidu has come to a halt. Representatives of Sikhs and representatives of Hindu Mahasabha Dr. Munje, Pandit Malaviya etc. accepted the recommendations of the Tribunal. However, the members of this arbitration board should be chosen by the Round Table Conference. The Sikhs and the Hindus opposed this suggestion (of Gandhiji and Naidu). The Muslims said that the members of the tribunal must be from among the members of the Round Table Conference and not from the people from the outside. The Sikhs, Munje and Malviya feared that if in the selection of the members of the Round Table Conference the names of Gandhi and Sapru come to the fore, they will recognize the mediation of the Muslims. Gandhi and Sapru are sympathetic towards Muslims. Their decision is not beneficial for Sikhs and Hindus. Due to this fear the Sikhs and the Hindus did not accept this plan.

This idea created a stir among the Hindu delegates who were Gandhi's devotees and supported the Congress. However, we came back disappointed at 1:30 in the night. We decided that if there is no agreement, we will have to go before the committee tomorrow, which is a shame. But Gandhi broke this mutual agreement. The second day, in the minority subcommittee held under the chairmanship of Macdonald Gandhiji made an irrelevant and unnecessary speech in an irritating tone. He said, "My attempt failed, I will not try again. It is not a special thing not to compromise on the question of a particular caste." He further said that they came to the Round Table Conference, so I could not compromise with them. Overall, Gandhiji's statement was an irresponsible one.

Representatives like Sir Shafi, Sir Petro criticized Gandhiji. However, my harsh criticism stung hard. I would not have criticized this hard, but his behaviour was very reprehensible. Hence, I could not stop myself from replying to him using bitter words. I know that my strong comments will be misinterpreted in India. After listening to me, Sir Shafi and MacDonald took a very harsh stand on Gandhiji. Following this, he adjourned the work of the committee for the time being. Later, the Secretary of India called me over phone. He told me that the Constitution would not be grant any recognition until the necessary rights were given to the untouchables.

I am an opponent of Gandhiji, yet I respect his simple and authentic approach. However, the way he tried to collude with the Muslims is not worthy of a good man. When I came to know about this, I felt disrespect towards him and got angry. Had Gandhiji directly opposed me, I would not have felt so bad, but seeing his petty policy I felt very enraged. That was the reason why I severely criticized him. I wrote an article in the English newspaper 'London Times' in which I severely criticized Gandhiji for his frivolous act. I sent this bitter truth to the leading newspapers of India. Although, this work did not succeed, yet Srinivasan and I thanked the Muslim representatives on behalf of the untouchable community for their refusal to protest.

Gandhiji said in a meeting, "I have not entered into an alliance with the Muslims against the untouchables." A list of this has been published that what conditions of Gandhiji must be accepted by the Muslims before he can accept their demands? This is also a condition prominently in this. In a way Gandhi assured me that if the minority community does not oppose your demand and even if the Congress opposes, I will consider your demands and whereas also compelling Muslims to oppose us, it is called gimmick. Not only this, many of his own followers are surprised to see the unjust and partisan policy of Gandhiji towards the untouchables.

Every day I receive several telegrams against Gandhi from the untouchable community from different parts of India. From this one can imagine the turmoil that was building up in the country. There have been some voices for my ban as well, but that ban is demand of upper caste Hindus who coined it and sent it in the name of untouchables by calling it a "national ban". This is what the kings and the emperors are saying. This means that the Constitution of the federation shall remain suspended for an arbitrary and unlimited period. For this reason, Sir Tej Bahadur Sapru also seemed angry with the kings and emperors.

A delegation from the princely states called on me. They came to know that I am putting forth my side at the Round Table Conference on behalf of the subjects of the princely states. They told their problem. I got enough information about their situation before they even said it. Hence, for this reason, for the benefit of the people, I took their anger on myself by arguing with the princely states. I know when the time comes I will definitely fight for the interests of the people but I do not have anyone's support. I expected that at least Gandhiji would, while speaking at Federal Structure Committee and protecting the subjects of princely states, would support it. However, I was very disappointed to hear Gandhiji's speech on the second day. Gandhiji's statement, "Don't insult anyone" about kings and emperors proved absolutely true. However, his attitude towards untouchables was altogether different. Just because these people were not as strong as the Muslims and also that they were not rich like the kings.

Any doctor experiments on the dead body of a poor helpless person, he does whatever he wants. Gandhi is also seen applying his truth and principles to the lives of poor untouchables. They should not get reserved seats. For this Gandhiji has put his life at stake while he was pliable in front of kings.

Gandhiji is a corrupt yogi who dwells in the kingdom of fools. He thinks that the kingdom of the kings-emperors will be like Ram-Rajya. However, it should be understood that all the princely states are staunch supporters of this safeguards and reserved rights. Their relationship with the British Empire is unbreakable and undivided. The Congress, which has passed a resolution for complete independence by breaking away from the British Empire, doesn't even understand this. However, this should be the shrewedness of Gandhiji's principles with regard to the untouchables. What can be bigger hypocrisy than this? Whatever his devout followers, the patriots may say; Gandhiji's litmus test was at the Round Table Conference. Other outspoken people like me also expressed the same. A gentleman said in sorry sarcasm, "Mahatmaji should be taken away from here, otherwise not only he himself, the country whose leader he is considered will all go into the abyss." Mr. Vithalbhai Patel and I met the day before yesterday. He had expressed his dislike regarding Gandhiji's policies. He said, "Gandhiji has created the entire Brahma scam."

It appears that the Round Table Conference will end either on 10th November or 20th November. This question would be asked everywhere that: Will this council end up achieving something or has something come out of this council? I'm afraid that the end of the Round Table Conference will be under very disappointing circumstances. If this happens then all the responsibility will fall on Gandhiji. The closure of the council could be beneficial for India, but such an effort did not happen at the hands of Gandhiji, this was the result of his half-hearted policy. Gandhiji did not had the clue that how real were the demands presented by representatives of untouchable minority? How intense was the feeling behind those demands? Due to this reason, those demands were ignored by Gandhiji. The result was that instead of solving the minority question intelligently it was neglected all together.

Such tricks were played by Gandhi that were not worthy of a Mahatma leave alone the common man. He used Chanakya policy on the pretext of solving the problems of the people, but he himself got trapped in this. I respected whatever Gandhiji said in the name of Congress about national interest and national pride. Even if I were not a follower of Congress or Gandhi I would have heartily supported those demands, but they did not allow me to have this opportunity. "It is okay even if we lose our life, but will not allow the untouchables to get the freedom."

Gandhiji took this bigotry to such an extent as to stop it I had to unite both the heaven and the earth.

The provincial government should be responsible to the Central government, I would have supported the Congress because I am of the Congress opinion. However, Gandhiji did not give me this opportunity because of his strange policy. The result was that the representatives of Muslims, Christians, untouchables took part in the debate till the question was resolved. But Lord Sankey felt that there was no point in raising it. Therefore, he postponed the work of the Federal Structure Committee.

Whether the responsibility is of the central government or not? this important question should have been discussed today, but it did not happen. No solution to this question was found, but Gandhiji didn't even discuss this topic. Thus Gandhiji's visit went in vain. The historian has described world conquerer Julius Caesar's invasion of Gaud province, "Caesar came...he saw and he conquered." Having written this much, the future historian put down his pen. However, the historian cannot write that Gandhiji won. Several people are disappointed by Gandhiji's failure. Had Gandhiji not come, the Congress would have been on course, now their friends and the followers are feeling so. Some people are speaking openly.

Some British devotees of Gandhi such as Harold Laski, were appalled at Gandhi's ridiculous idea of democracy. What will be the result, if the Round Table Conference fails? The questions are being asked regarding this. I think this question must have been brought to Gandhiji's knowledge. Gandhiji clearly said, "I will resume the non-cooperation movement." However, here before doing so, he has to keep two things in mind. First, the current government is of the Conservative Party. If Gandhiji had taken such initiative he would have been able to strike at their heart. By doing this Gandhiji would have to think about the minority society of India. Last time the minority community did not oppose the non-cooperation movement of Congress. When Congress participated in the Round Table Conference, the minority communities expected that the Congress would support their just demands. However, this hope proved futile. On the other hand, the Congress has resorted to unjust, casteist and illogical policy and now the attitude of the Congress has changed towards the untouchable society.

Not only from Bombay Province, but also from the Punjab, Bengal, Madras etc., telegrams against Congress-Gandhi are coming to me from all parts of India. In fact, Gandhiji is very delusional. Why do you oppose me when I am the saviour of so many untouchables? It is not possible for Gandhiji to resolve this puzzle in this life. As a result it is very clear that the Gandhi party and the untouchable community would be at odds with each other. There is a difference between me and Gandhiji as before. Gandhi's friends complain that I did not behave respectfully with them. My answer to them is that I am neither a devotee nor a follower of Gandhiji, therefore, hoping devotion from me is futile. The matter of the fact is that my behaviour towards Gandhiji is polite. I treat him as his competitor would behave.

Because of the point of view with which I look at Gandhi, they find my opposition unfair, especially to his devout devotees. I clearly made Gandhiji aware of the feelings of the untouchable society, but his delusion and prejudice never goes away. He says that 'I am the true representative of the Untouchables and that the Untouchables have no need for an independent electorate." When you are ready to give the free electorate to the Sikhs and the Muslims then with what face do you say that the untouchables will not get it. When this question is thrown at him, he gets irritated. The reason is that he is unable to answer the question properly. I met a French woman, named Muriel. She has great charm for Sanskrit language. Hearing the fame of Gandhiji, that woman had a lot of respect for him. The woman said, 'This morning I met Gandhiji and asked him, 'why have you adopted an inconsistent policy regarding the untouchables?' Gandhiji said, "If the untouchables are given free electorate, they will remain untouchables. Therefore that's the reason I am against giving free electorate to the untouchables." On this the French woman said, "If it were so, the representatives of untouchables like Dr. Ambedkar, etc. would not have accepted it." What will Gandhiji answer on this? The woman further said, 'He got a little angry. His behaviour indicated that I should leave.'

The day before yesterday Gandhiji had delivered a speech at an institution called "Institute of National Affairs". There too he supported the policy that he had adopted in relation to the untouchables. I also had a speech at the same institute on 10th November. One thing was clear from his views that it was his discriminatory policy to isolate the minority community. The end result was contrary to his wish though. Gandhiji's Chanakya policy was defeated. I would like to assure the untouchable community that Swarajya i.e. a fair share of the state power, is not about favouring the untouchables. Gandhiji's Swarajya will therefore remain a far-off ideal till we obtain our proper share of the state's authority.

India's national newspapers have launched a campaign of slander and misinformation against me. I have come across a lot of news in that context, some of which I have read and seen. I am not surprised by these reports. It is a matter of satisfaction that the untouchable community has remained oblivious to the opposition of the Congress. There was no awakening among them till date; however, now they have awakened. India's Dalit society has awakened to self-respect in opposition to Gandhi's just policies. Several messages have come to me in support of my demands from different parts of India and not only from Maharashtra. The Congress has sent four telegrams opposing our requests while taking along a few untouchables. But they cannot take our movement in the wrong direction.

Quotations have been sent to me from various newspapers in India. There are also quotations from the newsletter "Gyan Prakash". The actuality of the meeting of the untouchable community in Pune in the context of the Round Table Conference is given in that letter. An editorial has been written in 'Gyan Prakash' in the context of this meeting. 'Gyan Prakash' newspaper is not a one-sided newspaper like other newspapers of the Congress or the Hindus. But I am surprised even after reading the editorial of this newspaper, that a newspaper like 'Gyan Prakash', did not evaluate the controversy that arose between me and Gandhi. "Gandhiji is ready to accept a joint electorate system and granting reserved seats to the untouchables, but I am not ready to accept it; rather, I am stubbornly sitting for the right to have an independent electoral system." Today a couple of untouchable leaders are against me. They must understand what Gandhiji thinks. What is in the interest of the untouchables, an untouchable like me understands it more than an upper caste like him. It would have been better if Gandhiji had not come. However, his arrival has exposed his policy of favouritism. The day before yesterday some representatives of Hindi sent a letter to Mr. Ramsay MacDonald. People came to know about this from the newspapers. It was mentioned in that letter that "The British Government is ready to give India only the right of provincial self-government, but the Hindu people are not at all ready to accept the right of provincial self-government only." The first signature on this letter is that of Gandhiji. The truth of the letter is that on Monday, the 2nd November, Mr. Gandhi met the Chief Head. There it was asked whether giving provincial autonomy would work or not. Gandhiji had accepted it. No one came to know about this for two days. This secret was disclosed on Thursday. The Hindu representatives were horrified. Gandhiji was questioned a lot on Friday. Finally, after writing the letter, Gandhiji was made the first signatory to it.

The minorities made peace with each other. Gandhiji gave a strong speech against it. He said, untouchable society is a part of Hindu society. Therefore they are not a minority. Protesting like always, he strongly opposed the demands of the untouchables. Now it is time to give a befitting reply to Gandhiji. The role I played in the Round Table Conference was according to my conscience. Untouchables are Hindu brothers, therefore reconciliation should be done amongst them, such was the claim of Gandhiji. At the same time he made a secret agreement with the Muslims and said to them, “Congress accepts your fourteen demands. But you should act in such a way to ensure that the minorities and untouchables do not demand independent electorate.” I have a proof of this. And if any disciple of Gandhi wants to see this proof he may visit my office. Gandhi met the Aga Khan at the hotel to seek the support of the Muslims. He bought a Quran from the market and started persuading the Aga Khan. Then the Aga Khan said to Gandhi, “The untouchable society is very weak. They should get all the help and rights. They need it more than the Muslims. I believe that it would be appropriate for me to take such a stand on this matter and that is what I should be doing.” Gandhi returned disappointed.

Everyone's cooperation and support gives me the strength to fight for the political rights of the Untouchables. My movement and my work is not limited to Mahars only. Newspapers claiming national interest act as traitors and abuse others. Untouchables have given me maximum support without being afraid of these newspapers, so I have been doing something or the other in London. You strengthen the organization and we will move forward on the strength of courage and discipline.

Today in India, if anyone has to be called a traitor, the destroyer of the country, the destroyer of Hinduism, and the one who divides Hindus; it is me. When the Round Table Conference will think deeply, then they will have to accept that Dr. Ambedkar has done something for the country. If they do not accept it, I will also not give them any value. The trust of my community on my work is important to me. The society in which I was born, the society in which I am living and I will die here only. I will keep working for the same society. And I don't care about the critics.

I am accused that I do not work for the country. For the last hundred years, reformers, outspoken and taciturn people have been working to feed the people of their caste in the name of the country. These people have done nothing for my society. Then why are these people except me to work for the nation? Satyagraha at Mahad, Nashik, and other places have convinced me that the hearts of the Hindu people are as lifeless as a brick wall. They do not have the desire to call humans as humans and give equal rights to others. No matter how much you hit your head against the stone wall, in the end only you will bleed; the hardness of the wall will not diminish. Till date we did not have the sight of the Hindu deities, yet we have not died, nor did the dogs, cats or donkeys going to Hindu temples have turned into humans. If they can't touch us, then we also won't touch them either.

No pandemic has caused as much harm to us as this Hindu religion has done. We are within the folds of Hinduism since the past 2000 years. We have sacrificed everything for its protection, but still we are not worth a penny in Hinduism. The struggle that we have started is not just to get the temple thrown open to us or to drink the dirty water of the pond. We don't have to go to the Brahmin's house, we don't even have to share food with the society. We don't want the Brahmin girls. Are there no girls in our society? Why should we expect the Brahmin girls? Don't our women beget children? Actually our today's struggle is for political power. I don't like Hindutva anymore. My mind is thinking of changing religion. Wherever I go, I can live on the strength of my courage. But why do I only live in you? Because I don't want to leave you and go anywhere else? I want to tell you that I have to complete the work that I have taken in my hands.

❑

# Gandhi-Ambedkar Deliberation

On August 14, 1931, at noon, on the third floor of Mani Bhavan, the following discussions took place between the two—

Gandhiji – Doctor Sahab, what do you want to relate?

Babasaheb - You have called me to listen to your views. You say something; or else ask questions, I will answer.

Gandhiji - I have come to know that you have some hatred towards me and the Congress. I have been thinking about the questions of untouchables ever since my school days. You might not have born at that time. I had to make efforts to include these questions in the programme of the Congress. You must know this. These religious and social questions should not be mixed in the political programme. Such questions are posed by the Congress leadership. I have raised this question. Not only this, the Congress has spent twenty lakh rupees for the untouchables. Despite this, why do you oppose me and the Congress? This is very surprising. If you want to say something in this regard, then definitely say so.

Babasaheb - It is true that you have been considering the questions of untouchables even since before my birth. All elders have a habit of stressing on the issue of age. It was because of you that the Congress did not do anything special. You say that the Congress spent twenty lakh rupees for the untouchables, but it all went down the drain. If I had got this much amount, I would have brought amazing changes in the economic and social condition of my society. I feel that the Congress has no loyalty to its own programme. If this was the case, then the demand that Congress members must wear khadi as a precondition for membership would likewise have been maintained in order to end the untouchability. A home where neither an untouchable man nor woman works, which does not look after an untouchable student, or which does not supply meals to an untouchable student once a week. If the Congress had prohibited the membership of such people, then such ludicrous events would not have taken place today, and also the district presidents, who oppose untouchables entering temples, would have come to the fore. You'll contend that such a requirement is unjust because it will force the Congress to expand its strength. Then it would be appropriate for me to assert that the ethics should not come before numbers in the Congress; this is my accusation against both you and the Congress. Neither the Congress nor the Hindus inspire our faith. We are adamant about maintaining the dignity of both our own and the society. We don't trust Mahatma. Why should the Congress disparage me as a traitor in order to defeat my movement? (At this point, Babasaheb's expression deepened) He paused for a moment before saying, "Gandhiji, I have no motherland."

Gandhiji – You sure have a motherland. The report of the Round Table Conference is in my hands. From that report I came to know the importance of your work. You are a patriot. I know this.

Babasaheb - You say I have a motherland. But I want to say again that I have no motherland. How can I call this my country and my religion where we do not get drinking water and where we are treated worse than cats and dogs? How can an untouchable be proud of this country? Fearing injustice and atrocities, if we become victims of treason, then this country will be fully responsible for it. You recognize my service to the nation, which, you say, is beneficial for its cause. Even if this has happened, I did not do it because of love for the nation, but because my deity asked me. My people have been trampled underfoot in this country for thousands of years. While trying to give those people the rights of humanity, even if some damage has been done to the country by my hands, then it is not a sin. There has not been a single act that has harmed this nation. And the reason for this is my own loyalty. While giving the rights of humanity to my brothers, this thought should not be harmed even in my dreams. Then how will there be talk of sacrificing the interest of the country?

Gandhiji - I do not accept the political separation of the untouchables from Hindus. Thank you for your clear presentation. We know where we stand, which is good. (Babasaheb takes his leave)

❑

# The Poona Pact

In the Communal Award announced by the British Government, the untouchables were given the right of independent electorate. I was very surprised to see that Mahatma Gandhi was planning to observe fast unto death in protest against this. Gandhi ji had said in the Round Table Conference that independent electorates would be a hindrance to India's independence. Why didn't he sit on fast unto death for freedom instead of fasting for independent electorate? Why is this fast unto death only against the independent electorate, reserved for untouchables? Why not against Muslims, Sikhs etc.?

In order to improve their condition as soon as the untouchables moved their limbs, all the Hindus went berserk them. There is no open way for the untouchables to improve their condition because the Hindus have blocked it. In such a situation, the untouchables will have to be given special political rights, only then will they be able to see the way to improve their condition. Mahatma did nothing to give the rights. On the contrary, he opposes those rights and says that it is beyond his control to understand it.

I am a true well wisher of the untouchables. As per his views, the Hindus treated the untouchables like slaves, therefore they would never make the untouchables a partner in their rights. I demanded that the untouchables should get special political rights in the Round Table Conference. Gandhiji opposed this demand. Now that the untouchables have got those political rights under the Communal Award, Gandhi is opposing those rights by planning to observe fast unto death. This act of his is an obstacle in the interests of the untouchables.

Mahatma Gandhi had presented a plan before me in London, at that time I did not accept his plan. The reason was that Mahatma Gandhi or the Congress was not immortal, nor would they be able to protect the political rights of the untouchables in the future. Therefore, keeping faith in Mahatma, I cannot hand over the question of life and death of my society to him. The reason is that so many Mahatmas are thriving in India today, but they have not improved even an inch in respect to the condition of the untouchables. My people were untouchables for thousands of years and they still are today.

There surely are some reformers in the Hindu society, but they bore a little pressure from the upper caste Hindus, under whose sway these reformers plod their ideas and principles under their feet and become followers of the upper caste Hindus. We have had the bitter experience of this in Mahad and Nashik Satyagraha. To scare people by fasting and to make people realise that I am right, this act of Mahatma appears similar to that of threatening. If someone tries to silence the untouchables by threats or someone tries to make them bend over to his side, then this won't succeed ever. They should use the weapon of fasting for national work like Hindu-Muslim unity, unity against the untouchability. I hope they will not use this against the political rights of the untouchables. It is not our intention to separate the untouchables from the Hindu society. We only wish that they should be freed from the slavery of Hindus. They should suggest a more beneficial scheme for the untouchables than the Communal Award scheme.

I will make the political future of untouchables independent of Hindus, if this is the goal of Gandhiji's fast then I will strongly oppose it. I can never betray my people. I hope that the life of the Mahatma on the one hand and the political rights of my people on the other—Gandhiji will not put me in such a situation of religious dilemma as to whom to choose.

India's great personality Mahatma Gandhi! Even though his life is dear to me, but the rights of 6-7 crore untouchables are no less dear to me. I have to protect them first. I don't care if all of you together hang me on a street pole in an effort to protect them. The decision of the Chief Pradhan settles the main question of the Untouchables. This will not be acceptable to you or Gandhiji, then what do you want? Gandhi should tell this first. Considering how far the interest of the untouchables is protected in this? I will reply to you only after seeing this.

How much are these Congressmen trying to ruin my political life? After eliminating me these people will be your leaders, then what will happen to my society? What will happen by crying like this? Our ancestors were warriors. We will get killed while fighting, but will not back down from the fight. Come on, from tomorrow go to Bombay and villages and explain this condition to your people and defeat the Congressmen.

Four-five days back I was trapped in a terrible viscious circle. On the one hand was the political future of the untouchables and on the other the protection of the life of Mahatma Gandhi. But now I have come out of that circle. A lot of credit has to be given to Gandhiji for this. Gandhiji helped me more than anyone else when I was working in the Round Table Conference. But at that time if he had brought the ideology into focus properly, he would not have had to fast unto death. But what about them now? The question before us untouchables is that if you are making a

Hindu agreement, will you follow it properly? I hope you (all Hindus) will consider this agreement as a sacred partnership and act accordingly.

Sir Tej Bahadur Sapru and Shri Rajagopalachari worked hard to shape this agreement. Others also tried a lot. I express my gratitude to them all. But I do not accept the compromise that the country will be harmed by independent electorate and Hindu society and joint electorate will be benefited. The problem of untouchables cannot be solved by any political system. This settlement cannot solve that problem. As long as the untouchable class was ignorant and had zero self-respect, it would work as you told it and live forever on the land given to it. Now he is well educated and has a sense of self-respect. Now they will not be in your slavery. Not only this, if you do not leave the fantasy of your religious and social superiority and start behaving arrogantly with the untouchables, then the untouchables will stay away from you. Keep this in mind. You will do whatever you want to do for the Untouchables keeping this dreadful problem before your eyes. That's what I hope.

❑

# Eyes Filled With Tears

When Saheb had arrived after graduating as a Barrister, Ramabai's health was very bad. When DN Pagare met Ramabai, she complained - "Pagare Dada, what does your boss do? My condition is like this and he doesn't even ask about my well being. He doesn't even have time to look at me while coming down the stairs! On hearing this, Pagare went to Babasaheb Ambedkar's study room and said, "Sir, what is happening to you? Madam's health is very bad and you don't inquire about her well being at all; you don't even look at her while coming down the stairs. After this, what should I say to you?"

Babasaheb laughed at this and said - "What happened after all that this Mahar of Nashik got angry? Come and sit, calm yourself. Say whatever you want, but won't you understand me? Actually I am lonely, now you tell me what should I do? Should I continue barristership or do social work? And should I look at the house or the family? Forget about questioning, where is the time to see her while doing all this? Whatever little I earn from practicing law, I give it to her. Whatever is required for my expenses, I ask her. She has money. Shouldn't she herself visit a good doctor and take medicine? Instead of focusing on her health she worries about whether I had eaten or not! Now you tell me what else should I do for her?"

Even before this was completed, tears welled up in the Saheb's eyes.

# My Mission

I was born in an outcast society. I will dedicate my life for the progress of the untouchable society. I have made such a vow in my childhood itself. Opportunities to observe this vow came and went in my life.

If I had thought of doing well for myself, I would have got the opportunity occupy many prestigious posts. And if I had joined Congress, I would have got the best position as well. But I have resolved to sacrifice my life for the progress of the untouchable community. Now I am taking steps keeping only one goal in front of my eyes. To make any work successful one has to work with enthusiasm. I am determined to fulfill my goal. And to accomplish that task, it would be unfair if I resorted to narrow thoughts and actions. The government has kept the welfare works of Dalits in limbo for a long time. It must have pained my heart a lot to witness this. You would have imagined it.

❑

# Kind Nature

It was dawn. It was about five o'clock. Someone was shouting "Aho donde, Aho donde" from the door of our school in Parel. I came out and asked, "Doctor Sahib, how are you here?" Dr. Ambedkar replied, "Hey friend, I have come to have tea" and he began to climb upwards on the ghat. When the doctor sat inside, I asked - "How come here today?" The doctor told - "The maid who works in our Hindu colony came to pick me up at two o'clock in the night. She told that her husband was having diarrhea and vomiting since evening. She also took him to the hospital, but no one cares about the sick in the hospital. He is lying outside. She had come to request me to call Dr. Jivraj. I took out the car and took the woman along to the hospital. Only after this the treatment of the sick started. It was dawn, so I thought that I should meet Acharya Donde as well. That's why I called you."

❑

# Death of Maharaja Sayajirao: A Personal Loss

The death of Maharaja Sayajirao Gaekwad is a great personal loss for me. I can never forget his obligation. He arranged my travel to America for higher education, and hence, I am highly educated today. The untouchable society owes a lot to him. No one else did as much work for the untouchable caste as he did. He was a great social reformer. The social reform laws that he framed for the princely state of Baroda were even ahead of the laws of progressive countries like Europe and America. He studied social customs and also worked to remove its flaws. He was constantly working to improve people's lives. He became a symbol of success for the British in many ways. Despite being a Maharashtrian by origin, he always looked after his Gujarati subject. This truth is well acknowledged.

Sayajirao Maharaj's death has resulted in the loss of a notable personality for India. On the other hand, the people of the princely state of Baroda have been deprived of a great ruler. Maharsashtra also has lost a great person, a good son. The harbinger of social reform is no more, and the only well-wisher of the untouchables is gone.

❑

# 'No' To Second Marriage

Babasaheb was sitting immobile in the office. Pagare asked the reason for the indifference. At this, he replied, "Pagare what must I do? The children had a sad, sick mother; she also has passed away. Pagare inquired - "Who else is dead now?" Saheb replied - "Mukund's mother! Now there is no one to call the old lady in the house."

"You have sisters; you can bring any one of them."

Babasaheb - "They aren't around! Everyone passed away."

"Then get both the boys married."

Saheb said, "Okay, but where is the mother-in-law who will take care of them? In the absence of mother-in-law, both the daughters-in-law will keep quarrelling in the house."

"In that case if you marry again then it will be good. She will take care of the house and you too."

"What do you say, Pagare?" Babasaheb laughed and said. "You are well aware of my character. The new wife will be a reformer and well educated. She would say, 'let's go to the doctor, let's go to the movie, let's go to the party!' walking up the stairs with books in hands. I have exact opposite nature. She will then become upset, throw tantrums, and may complain that her spouse remains engrossed in books. Please explain, why should I be married once again. I won't get married again, regardless of what happens to this house."

❑

# Labour Minister

The Dalit class will not consent to a political state of affairs that demotes them to an inferior position. Along with the social, economic, and religious supremacy of the Hindus, now the burden of political supremacy too may befall on the untouchables. I will not tolerate that. Most of the people deny the upliftment and liberty, equality and fraternity of untouchables. There is not a single Dalit Tehsildar out of 100 Tehsildars and not one Dalit Patwari out of thirty four Patwaris. While there is just one Dalit in thirty-three sub-collectors, such is the proof.

What is my role? In fact, this country has not understood that. So let me take this opportunity to explain my role for this. Mr. Speaker, I solemnly state that whenever there is a conflict between my personal interest and the interest of the country, I will give priority to the interest of the country. I have considered my interest secondary. If I would have used my power and position for myself, I would have been in some other place today. Whenever the question of the demands of the country came up,

I did not stand behind others. My colleagues will testify to my role during the Round Table Conference. I believe in them. The British diplomats were stunned to see my standpoint in the Round Table Conference. According to them, I was the only one who asked questions which no one dare asked in the Round Table Conference.

But I will not leave any doubt in the minds of the people of this country. I am bound by some other loyalty and I will not permit any conflict to arise in that. By other loyalty means my untouchable class! I am born in it. As long as I am alive, I will not let any difference creep in. I want to strongly affirm in front of the legislature that anytime there is a conflict between the interests of my country and those of the untouchables, I will put their needs first. I also will not stand for the hypocritical majority castes. You must all be aware of my function. In a circumstance where choosing between the national interest and personal interest may be necessary, I will prioritize the national interest. But if the choice is between the interests of the nation or the society, I will support the interests of the untouchable class.

I am going to take charge of my new office from tomorrow. That's why I have presented the account of my last twenty years. Both the Muslims and the untouchables are both regarded as a minority; yet there is a huge difference between their position and ours. This has to be clarified. Muslim caste is richer than our caste. They were the rulers of this nation before the arrival of the British. They have made more progress than us. We have been exploited for hundreds of years. The condition of our society is very pathetic. We cannot compare ourselves with Muslims just on the basis of population. We should rely on ourselves to complete our work. We have to save our caste. This is my new appointment, so I am handing over my responsibility on the shoulders of others. I am not fond of rights (office). Even more important than my appointment is the need of a place for the representative of the Dalit class in the Governor General's

Executive Council. This tradition has now become a custom. This is a severe blow to Brahmmanical domination. My appointment is important. This tradition is not in favour of Brahmmanical domination. I believe this is a great victory for the untouchables.

There are many people whose opinion about me is not right. It is my nature to lead a lonely life and I spend my time in studies. Many people think that my behaviour with people is not right. However, I treat them fairly. But I want to tell you with confidence that I do not intend to insult anyone. My time is limited and I have a lot to do. And I have no aide.

Many Hindus look down on me with hostility. They complain that I speak language that hurts their feelings. But my heart is very soft. I have many Brahmin friends. The point is that I speak the truth. We are treated worse than a dog; all our avenues of progress have been blocked. Then why am I expected to treat Hindus generously? I also feel that the present Hindu generation has done nothing in this regard. That's why I control my emotions and try to treat my opponents with respect. My behaviour with my opponents is not that of dual nature, but it is their guilt that keeps troubling them.

As a member of the Viceroy's Executive Council, I had gone to Calcutta on official business. My friend Jadhav lived there on Upper Secular Road. I was his guest there. After finishing my work and having dinner at a friend's place, I came back to the Railway salon. The salon was scheduled to leave for Delhi the next day. The next morning, my friend Jadhav, his wife, and children were seen standing in front of the salon with their belongings, which surprised me a lot. They had seen me off in the night itself, yet how did the Jadhav family come here in the morning to see me off again? I was unable to figure out the mystery. Then Jadhav started saying – "Our servant has rebelled. He says that Dr. Ambedkar is Bhangi. He stayed in your house, had food. You also belong to the Bhangi caste. I am convinced now. My caste has got corrupted, my religion got corrupted.

Now whether we will be allowed to live in the locality or not, I doubt. Therefore, I thought of locking the door and sending the family to Bombay. This incident took place two years ago. This should have given you an idea of how unbiased Hindus are in their opinions of us. Perhaps the difference is that Hindus now call us 'Harijans' instead of Mahars or Bhangis.

❑

# Samata Sainik Dal

I am very happy to see the team of volunteers established in Madhya Pradesh. The first group of volunteers was established in 1926 in the city of Bombay. Samta Sainik Dal is a part of our movement. In fact, it is a powerful medium of our movement. The basic reason behind the establishment of this organization is to encourage the demands of the downtrodden class to get equality in the Hindu society. It is clear from the name itself that this has been established to achieve equality for the Dalits in the Hindu society. Today its aim is to achieve social equality at par with Hindus by completely separating it from Hindus.

The depressed classes did not have a meeting place to press for their political demands. The Congress organization was so arrogant that it did not allow any political party meeting to take place in Bombay. Our volunteers are ready to face this danger. They have saved our meetings from the atrocities of Congress volunteers by participating in politics.

I was preparing to go to the Round Table Conference. Meanwhile, a public meeting, in the name of untouchables, was organized by the Congress near my residence on the subject of my visiting the Round Table Conference. They were to announce in this meeting that I am not a true representative of the oppressed classes. I had told the organizers that I would have no objection if a genuine gathering of the oppressed takes place and in that a resolution is passed. But this gathering is not of the Dalit class. They had a meeting in the evening. At the last moment a group of our volunteers arrived and captured the meeting, cursing the Congress volunteers. Leaving the chairs, tables and bells, the Congressmen fled away saving their lives. Our volunteers brought chairs, tables and bells as symbols of victory. Our Swayamsevak Sangh is the strongest in Bombay. Till date no one has dared to challenge our volunteers.

There are some people who oppose the organization of such volunteers. They believe in non-violence; yet they oppose organization and show of strength. I am also a follower of the principle of non-violence, but I recognize the difference between non-violence and humility. Humility means weakness and it is not a virtue to cover oneself in the cloak of weakness. I have faith in non-violence. Saint Tukaram Maharaj has said two things while explaining the principle of non-violence: 1. have love and kindness towards all living beings; and 2. destroy the wicked. In the context of non-violence, the latter is neglected, due to which the principle of non-violence reaches a state of ridicule. Destruction of the wicked is an important part of non-violence, without which non-violence is meaningless. Power restrained with humility is our ideal. We do not need to be afraid of any hostility. Don't hurt anyone without reason. Help those who need your help in whatever way you can. As a result your serving the cause of people will be acknowledged.

At present I am a minister. Maximum attention is being given by the Central Government by keeping the interests of the workers paramount. The Royal Commission was also established on these issues in the year 1930; and that commission had submitted important information. If we go back to the history from 1930 to 1942, it will be known that nothing much was done in this regard. But from the time I accepted the ministerial post in 1942 till 1946, progress is visible. For the last 20 years there was only one workers' representative in the Central Assembly. However, in the new assembly you will see three representatives of the workers. On the other hand, there was not even a single labour representative in the State Council. But now a labour representative will be inducted.

Ten bills concerning the welfare of labourers will be tabled in the upcoming Central Assembly. I have drafted them. You yourself will see how efforts are being made to remove social and economic poverty from this country.

With political power in hand, a man can accomplish many things. Let me give an example. The Viceroy's Executive Board, in which I was a member, had 15 members. There, I was unaided and two years have passed since then. If you know what I did during that period, you will realise the state's power. Prior to my appointment to that post, the Central Government had not taken any responsibility for the education of the untouchables. But Aligarh Muslim University received 20 lakhs and Banaras Hindu University received help of 10 lakhs. Apart from this, annual assistance of three lakh rupees is being given to both these institutions.

When I went there, I started a help of three lakh rupees for the Dalit class from last year. In addition, 300 college scholarships (of Rs. 60 each) have been sanctioned. This year 30 students will go to England for higher education. Arrangements on this scale had never been made before, like I initiated. Now let's compare the decisions made regarding the job security. 20 per cent were reserved for Muslims, 8.5 per cent for Christians, but such a provision was not available earlier, in any measure, to Dalits. The only recommendation was to "pay attention to them." That is, our share was zero per cent. I had put this demand firmly in front of the government some time ago; ultimately, the government had to make arrangements for 8.33 per cent jobs for the Dalits.

When I became a minister in the Central Government, there was not a single untouchable appointed in our department from the bottom till top. But at present two Deputy Secretaries, one Under Secretary and three Executive Engineers have been recruited from among such candidates. Some people say that, "I only consider the interests of the Mahar people." If I am born in Mahar caste, what can I do about it? However, the complaint against me is completely baseless. Soon I am going to share information about the caste status according to the province. From the same report, it will be known that how many people are employed in which category of jobs. How many scholarships have been given to whom? Out of 28 servants in my department in Shimla, 18 are Bhangis. Among the people going to England there is one Gang, one Bhangi, and several Chamars. The purpose of telling all this is to demonstrate how much a person can accomplish with access to political power. Even being alone at work had allowed me to accomplish a lot. How much more I could have accomplished if I had another two or three people with me! I thus insist that battling day and night for political power is our first duty.

It is true that I am a lazy writer; though now I write more than ever. But it is also true that I do not get time to write anything else due to the engagement of the office. This is my real situation. Even though I am away from public life, I have never forgotten that even in such a situation my movement should survive. In my absence, you (Bhaurao Gaikwad) owe a big responsibility of social work. I have no doubt that you will succeed in this. During my tenure as Labour Minister, I have decided to help my society as well as others in every way possible.

The Labour Council was organized in Delhi under my chairmanship. Mr. Donde and R.R. Bhole were invited as representatives for that council. This is the beginning of my work. Such an incident had never happened before. Within a week, I have done many socially useful works. I have received your (Bhaurao's) letter of recommendation regarding Mr. R.M. Doifod. I don't know about Doifod. Some things I can do and some I can't. You know from my nature how strict I am in this matter. Doifod's case is such that I cannot do anything about it. His case comes under the Public Service Commission. Interfering in this matter is not appropriate. Such a situation is completely out of my control.

I have created numerous opportunities for the youth of my society. In such a situation, I can't impose on myself the additional responsibility to look after the affairs of individual candidates. Doing so will cause injustice to other eligible candidates. Therefore, I cannot interfere in this matter under any circumstance. And you know this very well.

I am very glad to see that some of our enthusiastic youth have prepared to run the Janata Weekly. I have a lot of experience running my own weekly newsletter; hence, I proceed very carefully in such matters. Overenthusiasm is not good. Running a newspaper is not an easy task. Monetary concern is a big issue in such a venture. Secondly, it is important to create appeal according to the reader's point of view, while maintaining the standard of the newspaper. I do not worry about its economics as it is not my responsibility. However, the second question is important. Who will be the editor of your weekly? or what is the person's qualification? all these are very important questions. I cannot give my consent to this plan until I have this information. And I have not even thought about its name. I cannot accept Kaivari (protector) or similar names.

❑

# Veda and Gita

I actually don't want to give a speech today. Someone told me that I should share my opinions on the plan of Sir Tej Bahadur Sapru. But, I don't want to discuss in this regard here. The Brahmins of Poona have expressed their grief about what I had said about the Gita in Madras. In my opinion, it seems reasonable to address them here. If a public gathering had been scheduled in Pune to hear my perspective, I would have spoken there. However, I don't have access to such a chance. Hence, I'm going to share my opinions on the subject today. Vedas are created by God, they are indestructible, their command should be followed; all this has been mentioned time and again. But, there is no historical proof of this. Apart from Brahmins, no one has given them any special importance or considered them as their scriptures. The doctrine concerning the existence Vedas was introduced much later by the Brahmins. The proof of this is found in the Ashvalayana Grihya Sutra. At that time Brahmins did not consider Vedas as proof; it is clearly mentioned in this. Even before the formation of social values, the public used to accept the decision of the Panchayat. At that time the Vedas had the fourth or fifth place. Shabar Swami has commented on the subject through the sources of Janamejaya wherein the perspective of Purvapaksha (antecedent) and Uttarpaksha (decendent) is detailed. Shabar Swami said that the Brahmins did not believe in the Vedas and that the creation of the Vedas was the work of a fool and lunatic. Such a claim has been made there. Buddha had never accepted the Vedas as proof. Buddha dealt a severe blow to the Veda-inspired religion. Buddhism was the religion of the Shudras, it did not accept the Vedas as authority.

I am accused of commenting on the Gita without reading it. However, these allegations are absolutely false. I've spent the last fifteen years studying the Gita, which is why I'm sharing my opinions. The Gita has nothing unique. In Gita, only three things are mentioned. 1. Are dying, killing, and violence sin? 2. Praise for Varnashrama Dharma; and 3. Devotion will bring about salvation. It is impossible to fully comprehend the Gita's message by relying solely on Gita itself. For this, it is also necessary to study contemporary (other) literature and then understand the Gita. It is known from this nation's ancient history that the Brahmin class and Buddhism engaged in conflict for almost two thousand years. As a result of this dispute, the literature that was produced during this dispute was not of the religious nature, rather it was of the political nature. The scripture by the name Gita was written solely to exert control over the nation's political centre.

There is only a partial translation of the Vedas in Gita. What kind of knowledge, after all, is contained in the Vedas? In reality, there are only two Vedas: the Rigveda and the Atharvaveda. I've studied the Vedas repeatedly. It makes no mention of morality or the advancement of man or society. Along with tantra-mantra (exorcism), the Atharvaveda also discusses what should be done when the wife does not love, how to manipulate other people's wives, how to steal money, etc. What purpose did it serve in a text like the Vedas, exactly? How Brahmins ought to interact with Shudras is also discussed in its Purush Sukta. It is stated that killing is the duty of the Kshatriyas. Although it could be necessary for one person to kill another person, but it cannot be his duty to do so. In the second chapter of the Gita (verses 18 to 39), which is based on Vedanta in which the soul is referred to as imperishable but the body is supposed to be destroyed for any reason — the specifics that we are accustomed to seeing. But stop and think for a second. In a murder trial, the attorney addressed the judge with, "Sir! Since the soul cannot be destroyed, why do you punish the guilty?" How realistic would this lawyer's claim seem?

The Vedic logic does not stand before the Buddhist philosophy. Through the Buddha's philosophy the social, psychological, and political revolution has reinstated the Shudras to a higher status. There is evidence that numerous Shudra kings ruled at that time. After the power slipped out of the hands of Brahmins, the Gita re-inforced the four-caste system; as a result power that was taken away from them was once again restored in the hands of Brahmins. What did Varnashram religion consist of prior to the Gita? In his work Purva Mimansa, Jaimini makes reference to it. Scholars like Charvaka and others have commented on the Vedic literature in addition to Buddha. Buddha exhorts people to abandon the Vedas and subservience and rise to power. Samkhya theory served as the foundation for Shri Krishna's creation of the Matrivarna structure. While the Gita's author recognised the four gunas and brought the four Varnas into harmony, the Sankhyakars recognised the Triguna. The gap between Sankhya Darshana and Gita Darshana though has not as yet been interpreted by any scholar till date.

I discovered four patches on this book while researching the Bhagavad Gita from a historical perspective. In my opinion, Krishna Varniya Yadav "Krishna" inspired a dejected Arjuna to battle. In the end, an epic was composed to honour Krishna.

The epic lacks all kinds of knowledge, including religious understanding. It had only 60 verses at that time. The odes for Krishna later evolved into the path of devotion when people began to regard him as a hero. Krishna was thus described to as a divinity. The Gita was altered afterwards and is now in its current form.

I don't want to place the blame on anyone. However, a belief is perpetuated that you won't receive any benefits from the world until you accept this book as proof. Shudras have received harsh criticism and neglect through this scripture. They have been accused of numerous things. The magnificent epic makes provisions for them to suffer inferiority complex and forever stay Dalits. Even if you compel me to take it as proof and call it a religious text, I will never accept it. My existence is based on the premise that I must first understand things myself before I can express it to my brothers. That which renders members of lower social classes childless, keeps them perpetually disadvantaged, and relentlessly destroys them is a distinct class that is unheard of elsewhere in the world.

❑

# Message to the Untouchables

On the occasion of my 55th birthday, you are publishing a special issue. You need my message to do so. It is quite terrible that in our society, politicians are revered as divine manifestations. Only the birth anniversaries of exceptional beings are commemorated outside of India. However, in this place, birthdays of both the Royal Purush and the Avatar Purush are celebrated.

The idea of celebrating my birthday has absolutely no support from me. I am a strong believer in equality and modesty. Then how would I endorse Vibhuti Puja? Vibhuti Puja is anti-democracy. It is reasonable to feel pride, admiration, and affection for a deserving leader. But I object to the leader being treated like a God. As a result, along with the leader, this will lead to the downfall of his followers. But will this be advantageous in any way? The politician should assume the position of an embodied man, then perform admirably and address his supporters.

What message should I give to my untouchable brothers, after all? Instead of giving a message, I would like to share with you a story from Greek mythology. Homer wrote a eulogy on the Greek deity Demeter, which goes like this:

The goddess Demeter came to the kingdom of Keliose in search of her daughter. She was dressed as a midwife, so no one could recognize her. Queen Meto Nyra assigned Demeter to take care of her young child named Mafun. Every night when everyone in the palace was asleep, the goddess Demeter would close the door and take the baby out of the cradle. After stripping him of his clothes, she used to place the child on cinders. This thing will appear cruelty to others. But she was doing all this lovingly with great effort to make that child a deity and gradually that child got the power to bear the heat of coals. He started growing up. But one night his mother suddenly came into the room and beheld the cruel experiment being done on her child; she pushed Demeter and lifted her child from the cinders. Though she got her child, but an ordinary son, deprived of god like qualities. After all, what does this thing tell? A man does not attain manhood or divinity without passing through the cinders. Man becomes pure only after passing through the fire; he attains divinity.

That's why Dalits will have to go through the fire of hard work and sacrifice; only then you will be able to achieve your goal. The Bible states that "Everyone gets an opportunity to run in the race of life, in which many are excelling." Why is it like this? This is because the downtrodden does not have the patience and determination to give up the luxury of respectability for the sake of a future. What could be a greater message than this Greek legend?

I want to give you the message to struggle and sacrifice. Keep up the struggle regardless of sacrifice and obstacles; only then will you attain liberation. Our work is sacred; we must have firm faith in it. There should be an organized effort to achieve your goal.

The work of the untouchables is great and the goal is big. Therefore they should pray with one voice, "It is our duty to save the society in which we are born. Blessed are those who understand this. Blessed are those who spend their body, mind, wealth, and youth in attacking slavery. Blessed are those who sacrifice. Blessed are those, who, regardless of death, distress, humiliation, tempest, pleasure and sorrow, struggle till the untouchables attain full humanity.

❑

# Three Goals of My Life

25 years ago, when I started in politics, I had three aspirations for myself. The original goal was to reach the Gyan Ganga stream to every untouchable's household. To a great extent, I have been successful in achieving this goal. Even though they may not be at the forefront of education, the untouchables will undoubtedly advance within a few days. In this, I have complete faith. The second goal of my life was to increase the representation of the members of the untouchable society in government jobs. You must be aware of the notoriety I have attained through this endeavor. My third life goal was to better the lives of my untouchable brothers who dwelt in the rural areas. However, I was unable to achieve my third goal as well as I had hoped. Therefore, there will be no change in the untouchable brothers' lives unless they move towards city. They remain attached to their upbringing in untouchable villages with their parents. They believe they have water and food. But respect for oneself is more significant than food.

They are treated like dogs in the villages, humiliated at every turn, and then made to live lives devoid of self-worth as a result of the insults. What use does such a village serve?

The untouchables who reside in the villages must leave and seize control of the waste land nearby cities. By establishing new villages there, a self-respecting existence should be led. A new society ought to be established there. All of the work has to be done there. They would not be referred to as untouchables or treated disrespectfully in such areas.

❑

# Love for Books

"I am handing over to you the dear companion of my life," Babasaheb stated as he presented the Siddharth College with his book anthology. "A person like me who was shunned by the society has been brought into the mainstream by these wonderful books. They are the only supreme lover in this universe. I therefore find it quite difficult to donate even one book to others."

I ran away from everyone and the world having been condemned by the society, but the books supported me. Giving the volumes to others becomes a matter of life and death for me. To ask for my library is to ask for my life.

My entire energy is revitalized when I read or write. I read and write all night long, but I do not feel weary. I have been reading constantly, which has sharpened my memory. I can quickly identify the pages and lines of any significant passage in a book. Knowledge is goddess of my worship. I continue to worship Her twenty four hours of a day.

There is no greater delight than spending a tranquil life with literature. Books make me happy because they make me learn and open my eyes to new possibilities.

I am unfamiliar with the skill of matching lovers. People claim that due of the intimidating appearance of my facial expressions, they are frightened to approach me. However, this is unfair. It is also true that I prefer the company of books to human interaction.

❑

# Research Work of Professors

Professor Reverend Father Heras, a scholar of mythological object revision and mythological history, delivered an effective speech at Siddharth College on the topic, “Article Reading on Mohenjodaro”. On the same day, Dr. Babasaheb Ambedkar spoke and threw light on the subject, "Revision work of professors”.

He said, Father Heras has very diligently read the article on the topic "Coins and Bricks found in Mohenjodaro". Everyone will be happy, proud and surprised. But I think the way Father Heras has revised a very important subject with a purpose that is not seen in our Hindi professors. Do they lack the knowledge or resources? What is the reason for this? We should think deeply about this.

I think—we get some money and our life is spent in comfort. Apart from this, our professors have no other ambition in life. In the absence of ambition, no concrete work is done by their hands. He keeps on writing comments on the textbook every now and then. Apart from comments, there are other important tasks, whether they are aware of it or not, who knows?

In the past, a professor had said—we professors are made of the education system currently being given in the university. Therefore, instead of blaming us, we have to blame the university education system.

On this Babasaheb said,—because of our university education system, it has become difficult to produce excellent professors. I accept it too. Many of our professors have to teach Shakespeare's plays or poems in the college. How will India benefit from teaching these to our young generation? Sometimes, when I can't sleep I read Shakespeare or poetry. But this is just to pass the time.

Ordinary level education is provided in our colleges. Education is imparted by Pantoji (Brahmin or Hindu teacher) method till BA examination. But it's not like that that he would not be able to reform himself. Now the city of Bombay has six major colleges offering arts and science education. Each college is affiliated to the university as per the present status, yet it exists as an independent institution. As a result, the same subjects are taught repeatedly by different professors in these six colleges. Due to which there is unnecessary repetition of work. Suppose, apart from this method, arrangements should be made to teach only History and Economics subjects in Elphinstone College and the professors who have to teach these subjects should go to Elphinstone College and teach that subject. Where seven eight professors of the same subject will come together. Then there should be division of work. One professor will lecture on ancient India, another professor on Buddha period and the Christian period, the third professor will lecture on the Mughal period, the fourth professor will lecture on the Maratha period, the fifth professor will lecture on the British period. This way the topic will be best shared. Every professor will get full opportunity to study his subject. As a result, you will get ample time for revision on your respective subjects.

Instead of waiting for other reforms in Bombay University, we should first bring simple reforms. Each university should choose one or two subjects, so that all the lessons of that subject will remain in that university. Instead of giving different salaries to the professors of all the colleges, everyone will have to be paid the same salary. That is, there will be no difference between salary in government college and salary in private college. When pay grievances are resolved and there is a better division of work, then the work of teaching and revision will begin.

In my opinion, professor should devote himself to study and teaching. The professor should hand over the housework to his wife. Professors should not take too many tasks on their heads and must be free from them. The study itself involves revision. Apart from these three tasks, the professor should not do any other work.

❑

# Entry into the Constituent Assembly

The responsibility of drafting the Constitution of my country fell on me, it was a unique event. The Constituent Assembly was formed to frame the Constitution of India. How my condition was at that time? You should know all this. The Scheduled Castes Federation was defeated in the elections of 1946-1947. There is no reason to be ashamed of this defeat. The reason is that at the time of that election the entire country was on one side and our party on the other side. On the one hand, there was a strong political organization and on the other there was an organization of minority untouchables facing them, that means its defeat was certain.

But it was not right to stop after losing. It was necessary for us to enter the Constituent Assembly from anywhere. The untouchable community is an independent caste in this country. It was declared by the British people. But the Cabinet Mission did not even mention the untouchables in its plan, it completely isolated the untouchables. Then I decided to go to the Constituent Assembly. It was important for me to participate in the Constituent Assembly for the welfare of the untouchable community. That I could not go to the Constituent Assembly, the Congress had put obstacles everywhere for this.

The person who says that I only am counted among the few nominated people of Maharashtra must indeed be a fool.

For the election of the Constituent Assembly, the Congress sent a letter to Mr. Jayakar, called Mr. Munshi, and sent invitations to many others. However, I was not called. They made several attempts to keep me away. That's why I had to leave Bombay and go to Bengal. There were no Mahars there, yet I was elected from Bengal. My opponents should keep this in mind. An opportunity was needed to uphold the political rights of the untouchables in the Constituent Assembly. It was a very serious incident. Due to the deep conflicts between the Congress and the Scheduled Caste Federation, the Congress decided that the Scheduled Castes Federation should not be let to enter the Constituent Assembly. The Congress had made it impossible for me to attend the Constituent Assembly. Finally, I found that way and I came to the Constituent Assembly from Bengal. I had one object in mind that I should be able to put forward rights of the Dalit class in the Constituent Assembly and ensure some facilities available to them in the state of Hindus.

## Untouchables

It was not my ambition to draft the Constitution of the country. Where it was difficult to become a member of the Constituent Assembly, it was impossible there even to imagine about some rights. It was decided that anyone would be allowed to enter, but Dr. Ambedkar would not be allowed inside. For me the doors of the Constituent Assembly were closed and so were the windows. Even the side holes were also closed. But for the works of public welfare, I kept stepping inside. Look at the wonder, the one who took a vow not to let me come inside, a huge responsibility was placed on his head itself. Man rarely gets the opportunity to do such a great work. It is a matter of pride for me, in the same way it is a matter of pride for you too.

Well I haven't done anything special. But from this work the Hindu public has understood one thing very clearly. For the last twenty years various allegations were being levelled against me. My party and I are not national, I am a friend of the British and a stooge of the Muslims. In fact these allegations are false. Now these people have come to believe that I am not like that. This is very important. The stigma of twenty years on our party has been washed away. Therefore, everyone should consider it their ultimate duty to protect the freedom of this country.

I have no doubt about it that the social, political and religious development of this country, will definitely happen if not today, then tomorrow. Today we are divided from each other politically, socially and economically. We are fighting with each other. I am a cantonment leader. Despite this, when the right time and right situation comes, this country will remain united. No power of the world will be able to come in the way of this unity. There is no doubt in my mind that even though there are many castes and many faiths in this country, we will be united. The partition of the country is the demand of the Muslim League. Nevertheless, a day will come when everyone will be benefited from united India.

I have no doubt about the ultimate goal of the country. But how can the resolve and co-operation of the country's mixed community of different castes to be driven on the path of unity? This is a genuine question. All the parties and castes of the country are eager to participate in it, therefore in order to please them, it would be a great feat if most of the parties accept their demands. Keeping the main needs of the public aside, we will give some facilities to our opponents. We will make more efforts and involve everyone on this front.

Once the front starts, it will march towards unity. Those who do not want to come with it, will also be taken forward with it. You should create such a possibility. If you want to know my opinion, I do not like factionalism. As per the 1935 law, I hold that the intermediate centre should be more powerful than the Center itself. For the last 15 years, the Congress' consent to weaken Central government of the country is beyond my comprehension understanding. There should be fresh efforts for a compromise between the Congress and the Muslim League. Why the parties should be given importance while deciding the future of the people? Now three ways are open—refuge, war or compromise! At present, many people have started speaking the language of war. But the very thought of solving the country's political problems by fighting makes me shudder. Many think that this war will have to be fought against the British. But I tell you with confidence that if there is a war, it will be against the Muslims, and not against the British. Conquering the Muslims or imposing on them the Constitution prepared by us is not going to solve this problem, because if you do this, you will always have to fight with them. Burke's statement - "It is easy to give power, it is very difficult to give knowledge." We have to show by our conduct that we have the power to walk ahead on the path of unity by taking all the stakeholders of the country together. You too have this power.

❑

# Marriage Letter of Yashwant

Dear Bhaurao,

You must have received my letter, in which I have written regarding Yashwant's marriage. It will be good if you come here. We can all discuss that topic together. I am very tired. I am going to Shimla or Mussoorie to take rest. Therefore you come soon.

Mr. Kawade had come here. He told me that there are three girls in Nagpur. Yashwant can choose any one of them. So you meet Kawade and Yashwant. I will come to Bombay in the first week of January.

I have received your letter regarding Yashwant's marriage as per his wish. Yashwant is independent. He dislikes Nagpur girls. What do girls look like? I don't know about it. But they were educated. It seems that Yashwant does not want to marry an educated girl. So he is giving priority to the choice of uneducated girl.

I do not agree with his views. I have not seen Mr. Rajbhoj's daughter. Their caste is different, however I will not refuse to the marriage. In fact, I do not believe in such things.

Yours

Bhimrao Ambedkar

❑

# Last Speech at the Constituent Assembly

The first meeting of the Constituent Assembly was held on 9th December 1946. Looking at that date, today the work of the Constituent Assembly is completed in 2 years, 11 months and 18 days. There were a total of eleven sessions of the Constituent Assembly during this period.

On 29th August 1947, the Constituent Assembly selected the Drafting Committee and the first meeting of the Drafting Committee was held on the second day i.e. 30th August 1947. Since then the work of the Drafting Committee went on for 141 days. The original Constitution had 243 articles and 13 appendices. Now in the final form the Constitution has 395 articles and 8 appendices.

Truth be told, finding and choosing the best of the best is commendable. For this the Drafting Committee feels proud of itself. If the Drafting Committee had not shown the courage to withdraw its faulty suggestions and accept better suggestions in its place, the Drafting Committee would have been discharged of its duties and would have been accused of arrogance.

The entire House, barring one person, has appreciated the work of the Drafting Committee and I am very happy with it. The Drafting Committee must have been blessed that their work has been praised so generously by the entire House. The personal greetings showered on me by the members of the Constituent Assembly and my colleagues on the Drafting Committee made me so proud that I cannot find words to express my gratitude.

When I entered the Constituent Assembly, I had no other objective in mind than the welfare of the untouchable community. Never in my wildest dreams had I thought that I would be elected to do a very important job in the Constituent Assembly. My surprise knew no bounds when I was chosen as the Chairman of the Drafting Committee.

The Drafting Committee had people more capable and experienced than me in age. I would like to mention Sir Alladi Krishnaswamy Iyer. Nevertheless, the Constituent Assembly reposed faith in me and elected me as its representative and gave me an opportunity to serve the country. For this I am indebted to the Constituent Assembly. I am not the only sharer of the glory that has been given to me for framing the Constitution. Sir BN Rao, the constitutional advisor to the Government of India, also has to be credited for the making of the Constitution. Similarly, the members of the Drafting Committee should also be given the credit for making the Constitution.

However, even more credit must be given to Mr. SN Mukherjee, the chief architect of the government. He has presented the complex information in simple and legal language. The importance of the people who worked under Mukherjee also cannot be overstated. The reason being, sometimes they had to work till midnight. I know all this very well.

If the whole public remained silent under the pressure of one party rule, then the work of the Constituent Assembly would have become infructuous. But there were some rebel members in the Constituent Assembly. I thank them too. The opposition of these rebel members gave me an opportunity to elaborate on the basic principles of the Indian Constitution.

In the end, I express my gratitude to the Chairman. The courtesy shown by you towards the members of the Constituent Assembly will be unforgettable. I am especially thankful to you for not allowing anyone to obstruct the work of framing the Constitution in the name of law.

I would not like to go into the merits of the Constitution. No matter how good a Constitution is, if its enforcers are inept, it will be like a false coin. Similarly, if the one who implements the Constitution is capable, then even a bad Constitution will prove to be beneficial.

In particular, the Constitution is cursed by the Communist and the Socialist parties. Why should they curse the Constitution? Is the Constitution bad? That's why they curse! It's not like that at all. Here the Communist Party needs a Constitution based on the principle of dictatorship. This Constitution is based on parliamentary republic principle, so they prohibit it. On the other hand, the Socialists wanted two things. Firstly, if they come to power, they want the freedom to nationalize, and secondly, they want the right to personal liberty.

There is a provision to amend the Constitution. No such stamp has been affixed that it is the final Constitution. On the contrary, simple, easy provision has been made to make improvements. I challenge that in these circumstances, the Constituent Assembly of any nation would have prepared such an accessible Constitution for reform? If this has happened, then someone should prove it and tell.

The authority of the Central Government will not be used in peacetime. It clearly states that it will be used only in emergency.

The second point is that when there is a state of emergency, the allegiance of the citizens should be to the Union rather than to the constituent states, such is the opinion of the majority of the people. The reason for this is that the Union state itself works for the collective purpose and for the defence of the nation. Therefore it is appropriate to give more powers to the Central Government during emergency.

I would have ended my speech here, but I consider it necessary to express my views about the future of the nation. India will become a republic nation on 26 January 1950. What will happen to freedom then? Will the nation defend itself or lose it again? This is the first question that arises in my mind. What worries me about the future of the country is that India has lost its independence once before. It was lost because of the hypocrisy of some people in India. This truth pierces my heart.

The British were engaged in defeating the Sikh kings, while the Sikh commander-in-chief, Gulabchand, was sitting quietly. He did not make any effort to free the Rajput kings from the clutches of the British. In 1857, when the flag of rebellion against the British rule was raised in many parts of India, the Sikhs were like other spectators passively watching the rebellion.

What happened in the history of India, will it be repeated? The mind gets scared by this question. Caste discrimination and religious discrimination are our old enemies. The new political parties which have been born and are going to form, their enemies are also going to increase. It is so true that if different parties give more importance to their ideology than to their country then their independence may again be in jeopardy or may be destroyed forever. We have all to be careful that such a crisis does not befall us. We should take a firm resolve to fight with our lives to protect our freedom till the last drop of blood in our body.

India will be a republic nation on 26 January 1950. This means that India will get all this from the day the state will be run of the people, by the people and for the people. What will happen to the republican Constitution of India then? Will India be able to save this Constitution or Destroy it again? In a country where democracy has not been used much, democracy is considered a new thing in that country. India is also one of such countries. Democracy in such a country, while going about its state business, is likely to invite a dictatorship to establish itself in its place. In emerging democracy, India can keep its exterior safe, but in practice dictatorship is likely to spread and it is also possible to happen. If democracy is to exist here, then in my opinion, the first thing we should do is that we should follow the constitutional way to achieve our social and economic goals. It means that we have to give up the destructive path, which includes law breaking, non-cooperation and satyagraha.

The second thing we have to say for the survival of democracy is that for those who are eager to keep the flag of democracy always high, John Stuart has given a message of danger, which is very important to follow. He says, "No matter how great a person may be among us? Yet one should not place the flowers of freedom at his feet." There is nothing wrong to express our gratitude to such a great man who served his motherland throughout his life. But even gratitude has a limit. Irish patriot Daniel O'Connell has expressed very poignant thoughts in this regard- "No man can express gratitude at the sacrifice of self-respect. No woman can express gratitude by sacrificing modesty and no nation can express gratitude by sacrificing her freedom."

India needs this dire warning more than any other country. The reason for this is that no other country has created as much storm as the spirit of bhakti or hero worship in Indian politics. The greatness of bhakti or hero worship in politics establishes dictatorship.

To maintain the existence of democracy, the third thing that has to be done is that we should try to achieve social democracy from political democracy. The existence of social democracy will survive only because of political democracy, otherwise not.

What exactly is social democracy? Social democracy i.e. liberty, equality and fraternity are the life-elements of every individual's life. These elements initiate unity. When separated from each other, the life essence of democracy is destroyed.

There is a lack of both the elements in the social condition of India. Accepting this, we should start building a social democracy. There is a similarity between these two elements. In the social context, the Indian social structure is based on the principle of ascending and descending order, as a result of which some castes are given higher status. From the day of 26 January 1950, we are going to get equality in political context, but we will remain unequal in social and economic context. How many more days will we keep procrastinating in establishing equality on social and economic basis? If we continue this procrastination for a long time, we will be putting our political democracy in jeopardy. We will have do away with this mutual difference at the earliest. Otherwise, these exploited, oppressed people will throw away the political democracy so painstakingly built by the Constituent Assembly.

We do not put into practice the principle of brotherhood. This is our second weakness. All Indians are real brothers of each other, keeping such a feeling in mind is called brotherhood. If there is any element that provides the nectar of unity in social life, then it is the element of brotherhood. If we have a true desire to attain the position called nation, we have to remove all the obstacles in our way. Because where there is nation, there only brotherhood is born. If fraternity does not exist then there is no meaning of existence of equality and liberty.

We Indians have a huge task ahead of us. My thinking is that some people will not like it. In India, a few people have enjoyed political power for most of the time. The rest of the Bahujans are the Dalit people who were living their life as per the orders of the rulers. Bahujan Samaj never got the opportunity to make its all-round progress due to political power being given to a few people. What is the importance of human life in this? Even the Bahujan Samaj could not realize this.

He now feels that he should work for himself and for that he needs rights and he is now ready to get those rights. The self-respect of Bahujan has now awakened. They have the motivation to do something themselves. It should not turn into class discord or class war. If this happens, there will be an atmosphere of disunity, rift and division in the country. This situation will prove fatal for the country. Therefore everyone has to follow the principles of democracy.

There is no doubt about it that freedom is a pleasant thing. But freedom has put a great responsibility on us. We should not forget this. After this, if some mistakes happen in future, then the responsibility will not be put on others. We have to accept them ourselves.

They are ready to run the government for the people. We have established the principle that the State should be run by the people and the temple in the form of the Constitution should be run for the people. If we want to keep that temple safe in the holy atmosphere, then we should not delay in understanding the negative things that stand in the way as hindrances. A State run for the people is better than a State run by the people. Such awareness should come in the public. We should not be negligent in removing this obstacle from the way. This is the only way to serve the country. I don't see any other way.

I am the architect of the Indian Constitution. The Pali language has registered its presence in the Constitution I have prepared. The second thing is that in the Rashtrapati Bhavan, the first step of the teachings of Gautam Buddha, Dhamma Chakra Pravartan has been inscribed. I brought this matter to the notice of Brahmadesh President Dr. G.P. Malsekar, he was very surprised to see this. Third, the Ashoka Chakra as a insignia of the Indian

Parliament has been accepted as the insignia of the Government of India in the Constitution. All this while I did not face special opposition from Hindu, Muslim, Christian and other MPs, I had explained so clearly in the Parliament.

❑

# Resignation of Law Minister

Till December 21, 1946, nothing was said from the Congress side. The discussion between me and Vallabhbhai Patle had failed before I left for London. There was no truth in the news of my joining the interim cabinet. There was no signal from the Congress side. If Congress had taken such a step, I was not going to take any step without consulting my party and without providing proper security to my community.

Calling me to the Secretariat 'Will you accept the post of Law Minister in the Cabinet of Independent India?' this was what Pandit Nehru had asked me. I gave my consent. I joined the cabinet. My entry into the cabinet was unconditional. Even after being a minister, I was not going to deviate from my path. I am that stone, which cannot be drowned by any water of the pond or sea. I will always struggle to achieve my goal. No one should misunderstand me and no untouchable should join the Congress. If you go to the Congress, you will dissolve like a lump of clay. So keep your organization strong and unbroken.

## Letter to Pandit Nehru dated 10 August 1951

My doctor and I are worried about my health. However, before the doctors have their say, I want to complete the work related to the Hindu Code Bill. Therefore, giving priority to this work, make arrangements to place this bill before the Lok Sabha on August 16, so that the discussion can be completed by September. How much importance do I attach to this bill? The Prime Minister knows very well the extent to which I am ready to bear physical pain to get this bill passed in the Lok Sabha.

## Resigned from Lok Sabha on 27 September 1951

I had been contemplating to resign from the post of Law Minister for several days, but it was not carried out because of a hope that the work on the Hindu Code Bill could be completed before the end of the last session of the Lok Sabha. I also recognized the division of that bill into parts and marriage and divorce were moral concepts extended in to these parts. I was expecting it to be the result of my hard work. But that part of the bill also came to a sad end, then there is no need for me to continue as a minister in your cabinet.

## Resignation Letter

When Pandit Nehru offered me the post of Law Minister, he assured that in future you will be given the Planning Department. But apparently he did not take me on even a single cabinet committee. This is the first cause of resignation. The second issue is that the government was indifferent towards the downtrodden. The third issue was regarding the Kashmir policy. By dividing Kashmir, the area with Hindu and Buddhist population should be annexed to India and the Muslim majority part should be given to Pakistan. The fourth difference was regarding India's foreign policy. India has more enemies than friends because of India's wrong foreign policy. Due to this wrong policy, out of 350 crore of India's income, 108 crore have to be spent on the army. Also there is not a single friend who would help India during emergency and the fifth point of resignation was the Hindu Code Bill. Nehru was so authentic, yet he should have shown the courage to finalize the Hindu Code Bill, but he did not do it. I did not drop out of the cabinet because I am sick but resigned due to disappointment. I am not the kind of person who would deviate from my duty by citing illness as the reason.

❑

# Illness and Second Marriage

As for me, I went to Delhi in a sick state and came back in the same state. Today itself the doctors have checked my health. They suspected that my health had deteriorated. You shouldn't worry about it. I stand firm even in this era. As long as my society needs me, I will live. I believe so. This firm optimism of mine keeps me away from despair even in this sick condition. I wish that I do not get more, but must get the required age.

The other thing about me is that my friend and medical advisor has definitely told me that I have a very high chance of getting rid of diabetes. But if this disease is not cured then the situation is confusing. Diabetes is a diet dependent disease. If there is someone to care about my daily food and insulin injections, then no one can tell if this disease will be cured. My friend says that if I am not ready for marriage then I should arrange for a nurse or a lady to take care of my house. I've been thinking about this for a long time. If a nurse or a woman is hired to take care of the house, suspicion will arise in the minds of the people. For this marriage is a more appropriate way. After the death of

Yashwant's mother, I had decided not to marry again. But due to the current situation, the time has come to break that resolve.

For this, it is not impossible to find a woman of your choice, but it is definitely difficult. My life partner should be educated. Similarly, she should be a doctor, as well as smart in cooking. Keeping these things in mind, it is impossible to find a woman with all the three qualities in our society. Similarly, it is difficult to find such a woman for marriage because of my lack of special relations in other societies. If the marriage is delayed, it will become a topic of discussion among people and the wicked will get an opportunity to defame me. That's what scares me.

I feel that by doing this I am not committing any moral crime. I have left no room for complaint, not even for Yashwant. I have given him thirty thousand rupees till date. Similarly, a house worth about eighty thousand has been given. I believe that no father has done for his son as much as I have done for my son.

My health is deteriorating day by day. I have not been able to sleep due to pain since four days. There is unbearable pain in the feet. Servants stay awake all night and serve me. Two eminent doctors of Delhi have examined me. They believe that if the leg pain does not stop, it will always be like this and will never end. I need someone to take care of my health. I am considering this announcement of the doctor more seriously than before.

My life has become so lonely that due to which I have no contact with untouchable Hindus and touchable Hindu women. But luckily I like a woman. She is from Saraswat Brahmin caste and I am going to marry her on 15th April.

I have come to Delhi on 11th. I feel a little better, but there is weakness. Earlier there was no improvement in my health. I was very ill in Delhi. On Sunday, 3rd April my condition was very serious. It's fine for now. At the moment I cannot do any work, likewise I cannot go out.

❑

# My Personal Philosophy

Every man must have a philosophy of life, for the reason that every man must have some measuring device by which to measure his conduct. Philosophy is nothing but the measuring device of his life. I condemn the negative Hindu social philosophy of the Bhagavad Gita. This philosophy is based on Shankaracharya's Trigun philosophy. The philosophy of Shankaracharya is completely opposite to the philosophy of Kapil Muni. Due to the philosophy of Shankaracharya, the descending order of caste and inequality has become the rule of the social life of the Hindus. The philosophy of my social life is contained in three words. Those words are — Equality, Liberty and Fraternity. However, one should not think that I have borrowed this philosophy from the French Revolution. My essence lies in religion, not political science. I have taken this philosophy from the teachings of my teacher Buddha. My philosophy is liberty and equality. Though equality is destroyed by unlimited liberty, excessive equality leaves no room for liberty. In my philosophy liberty and equality should not be infringed, therefore there is room for restrictions as a safeguard. But this restriction may violate guarantees of liberty or equality. I don't believe in this. Brotherhood has a very high place in my philosophy. The protection of liberty and equality lies only in fraternity. Another name for this is brotherhood or humanity and this is another name for humanity religion.

Taboos or restrictions may be broken, but brotherhood or religion is sacred. Brotherhood should be respected. Propagation of this philosophy of mine will be my living work. I have to adapt my mind. I will inspire my followers to follow this philosophy of life. Two thought systems govern the people of India. The political objectives presented in the Preamble of the Constitution testify to the primacy of liberty, equality and fraternity. But the social goals that are in the religion of Indians, they deny liberty, equality and fraternity. All Indians have accepted the political goal, it should be the social goal of all.

❑

# Academic work

After the end of the World War II, the first batch of untouchable graduates was going abroad for higher education. A farewell function was organized in Bombay to congratulate them all. At that time, Dr. Babasaheb Ambedkar had given guidance on how to acquire knowledge and how to use it? At the press of a button, an electric bulb destroys darkness and establishes the kingdom of light. Similarly every educated person should try to remove the ignorance of the society. To do this work easily, we should learn from the train engine. The engine prepares the entire train by adding coaches one by one and then takes over the entire train. Similarly, an educated person should do the work of furthering the revolutionary work of social construction and progress. If educated people in every society of India follow this path, then the Indian culture—bound hand and foot in the traditional framework—will be free. Only when this happens, India will again be able to move towards prosperity.

## People's Education Society

Babasaheb Ambedkar, while announcing the aims and policies of his educational institution, made it clear that the policy of the People's Education Society was not merely to disseminate education but to create such education as would develop India through intellectual, moral and social democracy. This is what India needs today. Everyone who has goodwill towards India should say this.

## Establishment of Siddharth College

Now your Principal has told that Siddharth College is still in its infancy, its tradition is yet to be established. That's why you have given me the opportunity to lecture. Taking advantage of that, I am going to lecture on the topic "My College Tradition". But before the lecture I want to say two words to the students of today. From 1937 I lost contact with the students. Since then I left the job of professor and chose politics. I get invitations to give lectures in many colleges. But I have decided not to accept the invitation. Siddharth College is an exception to this. How Siddharth College has to establish its tradition? I'll tell you that.

The name of our college is Siddharth College. Why is it named so? If I had talked to a millionaire, I could have easily got a few lakh rupees. If I had done that, I would have had to give the college the name of that millionaire. But instead of doing so, I named the college as "Siddharth College". You all know the name of Buddha. Siddhartha College has not yet established its tradition. It doesn't surprise me at all. You should not think that this small Siddharth College of ours has no purpose in these things. The college is named Siddharth College for some reason. Be careful, the college has been established in the name of Buddha. Buddha has told this goal in the Brahmajala Sutra. It has been told in that sutra that Brahma Darshan spread in India. These philosophers have faith in Brahman. His disciples told Gautama Buddha that the Brahmavadi philosophers had come to see him. They have established a new Tattvajnan (philosophy) and the main deity of that philosophy is Brahman. Shasta, what do you want to tell in this regard? We all want to know this.

I think the answer given by Gautam Buddha is worth considering. He asked the Brahmists, have you seen Brahma? The answer was "No." The next question was - Have you heard anything about Brahma? The answer was- "No." Then the question was, have you tasted Brahman? The answer was "no", then on what basis do you say that Brahman exists? Brahmavadis could not give any answer to this.

Now let me tell you about the second lecture of Gautam Buddha. Its explanation is found in the Mahaparinibbanasutta. Gautam was on the verge of death in Kushinar. He had disciples also. The chief disciple asked him, — "Shasta, you will not be able to attain Mahaparinirvana so soon. There are still many things to be done. You have not told anything in that regard nor have you instructed us." The answer given by Tathagat is worth considering. He said that "I lived among you for forty years. At present I am eighty years old. I am with you for so many years, still you are not getting proper guidance from me, I am very surprised. You may not have got ten all the answers from my side, I find it impossible. In these forty years, I don't even think that something would have been left to be told from my side. I think from your question that you have some confusion in your mind. You have not fully understood what I have taught you, I feel the same way. If you keep one thing in mind and then act accordingly, you will automatically get the answer to your question."

"If I am telling you something, it must be true, don't believe it at all. When your power of thinking and understanding, your reasoning power finds that thing worthy, then only believe it, otherwise reject it. This is my teaching."

What is the meaning of this statement of Gautam Buddha? This means that every human being should have the freedom to think. But this freedom should be used in search of truth and what is truth after all? The truth is that the five senses of knowledge and the five senses of action should accept the truth. This means that one should come to see, hear, smell, taste and take the proof of its existence, then only it will be true i.e. God.

Gautam Buddha had put this goal in front of his disciples. Siddharth College is going to follow this goal - 1. To find out the truth, and 2. To follow that religion that will teach humanity.

In which direction is the modern thought system flowing? This is known to me. Let me tell you that I am no stranger to the philosophy of Karl Marx. His religious views are also not unknown to me. They say that religion is an opium. But I do not agree with his statement. I think that finding out the truth is Satyadharma. Truth and power are opposite things. The scriptures also do not accept perfection in any way. That's why there is nothing completely pure in the world.

Dharma means Truth, we should understand that "Nahi Satyat Paro Dharmah (There is no religion higher than Truth)" should be our aim. We should never make others sad. This should be the true lesson of our religion. Man should have complete freedom in the work of Satyashodhan (seeking truth). This is also the aim of our college.

## Milind College

Milind (Menander) was a Greek king. He was proud of his scholarship. Scholars like Greeks will not be found anywhere in the world. Once he felt that I should debate with a Buddhist monk. But no one was ready to argue with Milind. Nagsen Sadhu got ready after a lot of efforts. The monk accepted Milind's invitation.

Nagsen was a Brahmin. He left his parents' home at the age of seven. Later, he became a Buddhist monk. There was a debate between Nagsen and Milind, in which Milind was defeated. A book has been published on this duologue. The name of this book in Pali language is "Milind Panha". This book has been translated by the name "Milind Prashna". I wish that teachers and students study this book. It has been told in this book that what should be the qualities of a teacher? That's why the People's Education Society and I have named this college as "Milind Mahavidyalaya" and the college campus as "Nagasen". Milind was defeated and later became a Buddhist. That's why I take on his name. I think it's a perfect name.

It is completely wrong to adopt a name of a rich businessman because he gave financial help to an educational institution. Another reason for giving this name to the college is that like food, education is also necessary for every human being. Everyone should get the benefit of this. The first person to announce this liberal idea was Gautam Buddha. At that time innumerable people were kept in the darkness of ignorance for hundreds of years. Tathagat Buddha and his disciples began to educate them. It is natural to remember him today.

2100 students study in Bombay's Siddharth College and 600 students study in this college. I have carried a lot of burden of this college. Shri Shankarrao Dev has quoted a verse from the Dhammapada on naming the college "Milind". That is - "amhodhen jayet krodham". Anger must be conquered by no anger. I get very angry, everyone knows this. Sri Deva says - "One should swallow anger." I think Deva's study is incomplete. Tathagata has lectured on agitation. If Deva had read it, he would not have said this. Man is angry, yet one should not comment on him. There are two types of attachment/anxiety - 1. hateful 2. loving. The butcher takes the axe, his attachment is malicious, while a mother slaps her child, what would it be called? Her attachment is loving. Be a virtuous son, that's why she slaps her son. My attachment is also loving. You should also behave with sense of equality. I don't care about critics. Whatever has been achieved, has been achieved by fighting.

Earlier only the Brahmin caste used to get education. We did not know how to get education. We had a great desire to acquire knowledge. But the Brahmins did not allow us to gain education. But Tathagat has broken that bond. Once a Lohit Brahmin asked Buddha why do you teach knowledge to everyone? Then Gautama Buddha replied, "Just as man needs food, similarly everyone needs knowledge." This work was first started by Gautama Buddha. Knowledge is like a sword in a way. The sword is double edged. He goes on killing the wicked with the sword and also protects one from the wicked. That is why it has been said – "Swadeshe Pujyate Raja, Vidvan Sarvatra Pujyate." (There can never be any comparison between a scholar and a king because a king gets honour and respect only in his own kingdom and a scholar gets respect and prestige everywhere).

You have all come to gain knowledge, but in my opinion only knowledge cannot be pure. Tathagat has told about knowledge as well as meaning of knowledge. Pragya means love towards mankind and friendship means one should have a sense of belonging towards all living beings. Only then can knowledge be useful.

Every student of Milind College should build his character according to the five principles of learning, wisdom, pathos, modesty and friendship. If you have to tread this path alone, then you should do it with patience and devotion. We should move ahead on the path which we find worthy according to our discretion.

## Importance of Education

Dr. Babasaheb Ambedkar established Milind Mahavidyalaya in Aurangabad in 1950 through the People's Education Society. The foundation stone of the college building was laid on 1 September 1951 by the first President of India, Dr. Rajendra Prasad.

Babasaheb Ambedkar explained the importance of education on the President's welcome speech and said, "Being from the lower class of Hindu society, I know the importance of education. What should be done to improve the status of lower class people? Considering this, many economic questions are often mentioned. It is often believed that their progress lies in solving economic questions. But it would be a big mistake to believe this. For the upliftment and emancipation of the lower classes in India, as in ancient times, they should not be kept busy in the service of the upper castes by making free arrangements for food, drink, clothes etc. They have to be uplifted by freeing them from the toxic tradition of discrimination between human beings. For this, by inculcating discretion in the minds of the lower level people, they have to be told the importance of individual and national life. How have they been cheated in the social system in which they were living till date? All this has to be explained. This work is not possible in this country without higher education. In my opinion, the only and best solution to all the social problems of India is the spread of education.

❑

# Doctorate Degree

I have decided to go to America. I don't like going to Columbia University to get my LLD degree. After coming from Bombay, my health deteriorated further. Even after getting treatment, there is no benefit. That's why my health has become the cause of your worry and sorrow. But now I have stopped worrying. I don't think my health will improve like before. Tathagat Buddha has said, "Whatever is born is sure to perish." So you should not worry. Instead of worrying about my health, you people get ready soon to take up the responsibility of social work placed on my head. I believe that I will not be able to live much longer.

My departure to America on 5$^{th}$ June 1952 is getting very close. I have angry nature. There have been heated debates on many issues with the people in power. However, let no one think that I will speak harshly about India abroad. I have never rebelled against the country. I have thought only good of my country in my heart. At the time of the Round Table Conference, I was 200 miles ahead of Gandhiji in the national interest.

❑

# Bombay Belongs to Maharashtra

Maharashtrians comprise the majority of workers in the industrial sector of Bombay city and the majority of workers in all office sectors. This class always works hard for the development of the city. The number of Parsis working in textile mills and office work is very small. It is my clear opinion that Bombay will not develop without Maharashtrian people. The tripartite scheme of Maharashtra state formation is in the form of Western Maharashtra, Central Maharashtra and Eastern Maharashtra. Their respective capitals will be Bombay, Aurangabad and Nagpur. As suggested by the erstwhile Maharashtra State Reorganization Board, part of Vidarbha would include the districts of Nagpur, Bhandara, Wardha, Yavatmal, Akola, Amravati, Buldhana and Chanda. Central Maharashtra will include Aurangabad, Parbhani, Nanded, Beed, Osmanabad, Nashik, Dangs in Solapur district, Ahmednagar, East and West Khandesh and Marathi areas adjacent to Karnataka. The rest will go to West Maharashtra, which will include Thane, Colaba, Ratnagiri, Pune, North and South Satara, Kolhapur, Belagavi and Karwar districts. Economically and culturally, three parts will be possible and as a result of this scheme, the hopes and aspirations of the people of these divisions will be fulfilled.

In my opinion, the demand for a united Maharashtra is unjustified. The reason is that the backward districts of Marathwada will not be able to move forward in United Maharashtra, due to which a situation of anarchy may again arise in United Maharashtra. If there is a desire to develop backward Marathwada, then it would be appropriate to make Marathwada independent. According to my Tri group plan, if there are three states in Maharashtra, then those states will prove to be efficient from the point of view of business. Along with this, the public will also get opportunities for progress.

Being educationally backward, there is a great need for an independent university in Marathwada.

❑

# Works of Saints in Maharashtra

The supremacy of one class over the other, this is the origin of Chaturvarna. There were many rebellions against the Chaturvarna system, in which the rebellion by the saints of Bhagwat religion of Maharashtra is prominent. This rebellion was completely different. Like other human beings, Brahmin is also a human being, then Brahmin is the best or God is the best? It was such a rebellion. The Brahmin man is the best or the Shudra man is the best? Sages and saints did not bother to solve this question. Sages and saints were victorious in this rebellion and Brahmins recognized the superiority of the devotees.

However, this rebellion was of no avail in terms of destroying the Chaturvarna system. It is not that the cover of devotion gives meaning to humanity. The value of humanity is self-evident. The saints did not fight for this cause. As a result, the pressure of Chaturvarna remained. The rebellion of the saints had side effects. You become a devotee like Chokhamela, then we will accept you. This new tactic of exploiting the downtrodden class fell into the hands of the Brahmins. The hands of those who rebelled among the Dalits loosened. This is the experience of Brahmins.

Communal people exaggerate the miraculous legends of sages and saints. These people ridicule the compassionate, just, egalitarian and liberal thoughts of sages and saints. The reason is that caste ego has dominated them. The people of Ramdasi sect are already caste conscious. The founder of this tradition is suffering from the pride of varna supremacy.

I was attracted to the saint literature of Maharashtra in my youth. How helpful is literature in strengthening the morality of man? I can tell this very well.

❑

# Do You Think I Am A Litterateur?

Vidarbha Literature Association, Nagpur

May 1954

Writers and Scholars!

I got an opportunity to visit your literary institution today. That opportunity has come by on the request of two litterateurs. One is yours and one is ours. Gajananrao Madkholkar is yours and Narayanrao Shende is ours. This difference is felt. But you have created this difference in life, not us. We are fighting to end this discrimination, not you. I got invitation from Mahar and Brahmin, I found this meeting auspicious. So I have agreed to visit this literary institution. I don't take anything lightly, I check thoroughly. I know whether the coin is real or fake. There is a fear of being cheated. Many such deceptions have happened with us umpteen times. But now this will not happen to us because we have become careful now.

That is why there should be no difference in life. Welfare can be achieved only by always being aware and efficient, such literature should be created. Literature may be of any type, it should be irrigated with the nectar of words, only then it will be called literature, it will be considered as protector literature. Saint Gyaneshwar says – "The word should have so much power that it can conquer even the nectar."

The writer should understand the meaning of Daham (tenth) and Shatam (hundred) very well. Daham should not be burnt and Shatam should not be given refuge and death. But the ego makes all this happen. Ego is very dangerous in literature. It lacks patience. Life should be developed and upgraded only by the speed of literary practice and the touch of a generous heart. Only then he becomes a reader, a writer. Today's litterateur tries his best to take Daham's step ahead, then pulls Shatam hundred steps back. He sometimes plucks the beautiful flowers of the garden and sometimes steals them away. But those flowers are not offered at the feet of the deity. One who makes a beautiful garden does not become a skilled gardener.

But I am a gardener. I can understand Gyaneshwar's "Gyaneshwari", Tukaram's "Gatha", Lokmanya Tilak's "Gita Rahasya", Haribhau Apte's "Pan Lakshat Kon Gheto?" novel, "Kala Pani" by Savarkar, "Sushilena Dev" by Vaman Malhar Joshi, "Shyamchi Aai" by Sane Guruji, "Daulat" by Phadke, "Hridayachi Haak" by Khandekar, "Bhangalele Deul" by Madkholkar, "Tutari" by Keshavsut, Yashwant's "Aai" and Gadkari's "Footkam Naseeb". But I don't understand today's story, poetry, drama.

Today the literature which develops the life of the society and the nation is not being created. Our independent country is in dire need of unity and fraternity. Unity and brotherhood is the focal point of our nation. Without them, a strong union power will not be built. That's why it is absolutely necessary to build a humanistic science from literature and art. For that there should be a wave of national utility revolution in the field of literature. Presently we are seeing that the wall of literature seems to be weakening. The crop is high, but lacks essence. Today we are hungry for knowledge, we should fulfill it. Poet Keats says- "Heard melody is sweet but that unheard is the sweetest." Experience should come in this way. Saint Gyaneshwar has said in Pasaydan- "May the world be benefited by the sacrifice made by literature. May all mankind be happy, blissful and all be resolved." The writers should follow these indications.

We neglect our life, our duty and our culture. If we reflect being introvert, then it will be known that our life values and cultural values are deteriorating, due to which an ugly picture is visible. Whatever may be the reason, but we are going down the path of degradation, It is visible. Hence, litterateurs should be careful about cultural life and readily preserve the cultural values.

The Sita of your story-novel is now crossing the Lakshman Rekha. Draupadi is being stripped naked in Duryodhana's court and Dushyant does not care about Shakuntla. She is in exile. That's why I want to tell the mantra (formula) to writers –

Innovate liberal life values and cultural values in your literature. Don't keep your goal small, make it big. Instead of keeping your coins imprisoned in four walls, take them to remote villages, so that the darkness there may be dispelled. There is also a world of neglected, downtrodden and indigent people in our country, never forget this. Understand their plight and pain very well and try to improve their life through your literature, this will be true human service.

❑

# Dog and Babasaheb

What happened one day that the Babasaheb's pet dog was neither eating nor drinking anything. Babasaheb got very worried. The dog was being treated and taken care of in every way. Baba hugged him and said with compassion, "what has happened to you? Why this Satyagraha? Why is this fasting? Tell something!" Babasaheb's eyes had become moist. His beloved and trusted dog was neither eating nor drinking anything, due to which Babasaheb also abstained from food for two days. Babasaheb was very happy when the dog ate bread with milk on the third day in the morning. Such was Babasaheb Ambedkar's love for all living beings!

❑

# My Personality Is Made of This

For the position I have reached today, I must have some inborn qualities, no one should think like that. Actually I have achieved this height by my own efforts.

## First teacher Buddha

I have three gurus, because of them only there has been a revolution in my life. The credit of my progress goes to them only. My first teacher is Gautam Buddha. Dada Keluskar was a learned friend of my father. He wrote the character of Gautam Buddha. Keluskar Guruji presented Buddha Charitra to me at a function. After reading that book, I had had a different experience. There is no place for high and low in Buddhism. After reading Buddha's character I lost my faith in Ramayana, Mahabharata, Gyaneshwari etc., I became a follower of Buddhism. There is no religion like Buddhism in the world. If India has to survive, it will have to embrace Buddhism.

## Second Guru Kabir

My second Guru is Saint Kabir. There was not even an iota of sense of discrimination in him. He was a Mahatma in true sense. I call Gandhi Mr. Gandhi. I receive many letters, in which it is requested that I should call Gandhiji as Mahatma Gandhi. But I did not give importance to their request. I want to place the teachings of Saint Kabir in front of these people.

## Third Guru Phule

"*It is difficult to be a human being, so how to become a monk*?"

My third guru is Mahatma Jyotiba Phule. I got his guidance. Due to his efforts, the first girls' school was opened in this country. My life has been shaped by the teachings of Tathagat Gautam Buddha, Saint Kabir and Mahatma Jyotiba Phule.

## Three Revered Gods

Like three gurus, I have three gods to worship. My first worshipful is Goddess Vidya. Nothing is possible without knowledge. The majority of the society in this country is illiterate. The Buddha was called Shudra by the Brahmins, but there is no caste in Buddhism and no prohibition to acquire education. Man needs knowledge like food. Brahmins have prohibited others from seeking knowledge. They have muted the voice of the students. The result of this is that today 50 per cent people in the country are illiterate. Buddhism is in Brahmadesh, 90 per cent of the people there are educated. This is the difference between Hinduism and Buddhism.

I love books with the same yearning that a true lover loves his beloved. Enemy should also be accepted, such knowledge should be imparted. If you come to my Delhi residence, you will see my collection of 20,000 selected books. I humbly want to ask if anyone else would have seen such wealth?

Self respect is my second god. It is true that I am always humble. Humility does not mean helplessness. I understand compulsion as an excuse. Man should live with self-respect. I have set the goal of social work before my eyes. But the thought of depending on others to play my part never crossed my mind. I did not come under the guise of a job for social work. I spent many years in a 10x10 room in Parel-Mumbai. I ate Kanaki's bread and Kanki's rice (broken/low cost grains), but never took a bag (money/fund) from anyone for myself. I had cordial relations with the Viceroys and Governors of this country, but I never appealed to them for me. To help others, I got them to do that work.

My third worshipful deity is modesty. I have never harmed or done wrong to anyone. You will not see a single such example. I could have been a Supreme Court Justice. But can social work be done by getting stuck there? I act according to my conscience. I never thought about how others would feel. I do not believe in God. I consider Sheelacharan (good conduct) as my deity.

❑

# Morality Matters

I am a virtuous and moral person of high order. My whole public life is based on this reputation. Enemies fear me because of my sacred character. There is fear in their hearts and minds about me. I can never be ready to tarnish this auspicious reputation. If my reputation is destroyed, then the whole purpose of my life will be destroyed. My people, for whom I have sacrificed everything, those who consider me as a deity, all will lose faith in me.

I am a very tough person. Yet I am as calm as water and as tender as grass. But when I am angry it becomes very difficult to control me. I am a man of silence. I am often accused of not talking to women. But I don't often talk to men either. I'm a self-absorbed person. Sometimes I speak incessantly, sometimes I don't utter a word. Sometimes I'm very serious, sometimes I'm jaunty. I'm not a sarcastic person. The luxuries of life do not gravitate me. My associates will have to put up with my firm demeanour, harshness and stoicism. Books are my favourite thing. I love books more than I love my wife and children.

I am a great fighter who fights for the progress and emancipation of women. I have fought to uplift the status of women and achieve it. I am very proud of this.

I have a special attachment to literature, especially literature of life. The life of every man and woman is brief. The path by which they complete their life cycle is narrow. That's why everyone's experience is limited. This limited experience gives rise to narrowness and contraction. There are many such people in life, whose experience is different from the other person. Unless a person is familiar with his experience, he cannot develop his life. Tolstoy is not my hero nor any writer is my hero. My ideology very serious. I take the statement of any author only if it is appropriate, accept it and build my personality. But no matter how great someone is, I do not follow them, this is my fundamental thinking.

❑

# Different Religions

Jesus Christ says in Christianity - consider me as the son of God, then I will take you to God. If you are not ready to accept this, then you will not be able to go to God. Some Christians say that if Jehovah is your God, then he has not asked you to marry; and if this is true, then how can it be believed that Jesus Christ is the son of God? In Muslim religion, Prophet Muhammad teaches that I am the only messenger of God, as well as I am the first and the last messenger. You have to accept this first, then only I can take you to God. But those who are not ready to accept this, will be considered traitors.

In Hinduism, when there is a loss of religion, when religion is destroyed or unrighteousness reigns, then Lord Vishnu incarnates and establishes religion. Assuming this, will any man sit silently with folded hands? On the one hand, it is said that if a man does good deeds, he becomes Narayan of a man. On the other hand, the man has nothing to do, Narayan will do everything. After all, what is their point? With this kind of illogical ideology, man cannot perform his duty.

In contrast to this is the teaching of the Buddha. The religion of Buddha is the only true human religion. The Buddha never said that he was an incarnation of God, that he was a messenger of God, or that he was the only son of God. Therefore, by becoming a human religion, Buddhism has been created for the complete development of human beings. This religion is for the welfare of every person. In this religion every person has complete freedom and only that which is acceptable to humanity and conscience is considered acceptable.

Just as there were rules for conducting the business of the Parliament, similarly the rules were followed in the Buddha Sangha. If a person wants to join the Buddha Sangha, he must first become a disciple of a guru (Buddha). The monk kept a close watch on the behaviour and conduct of the visitor candidate and if they were convinced, he was recommended. Only then the visitor was enrolled in the Sangh. Later, a secret ballot (by writing on a palm leaf) was conducted for him by putting a vote in the box. If there was not even a single vote against him, only then the candidate was given entry into the Sangh.

❑

# Similarity Between The Teachings of Buddha and Jesus Christ

Scholars named Professor Anasaki and Mr. Edmonds have authored an important book on the comparative study of the teachings of Buddha and Jesus Christ. From this it can be seen that the teachings of Jesus Christ are the teachings of Buddha. He has shown a similarity between the vision of Buddha on the one hand and the vision of Christ on the other. For many years I had this idea in my mind to translate this book in Marathi and bring it before the public. I have kept this book very carefully. I do not give this book to anyone. But due to the extreme insistence of some people, I gave a part of the book to a friend of mine to read. But he missed that part. I feel very bad for what happened to this favourite and rare book of mine. After all, I had to buy that part of the book. I got that part at a bookseller by chance.

❑

# Revival of Buddhism

During my tenure in the Parliament, I have done some work for the revival of Buddhism. I am the architect of the Constitution of India. I have included the plan for the upliftment of Pali language in the Constitution. Secondly, I have had the first step of Gautam Buddha's teachings 'Dhamma Chakra Pravartan' inscribed in the Rashtrapati Bhavan. I told this to the president of Brahmdesh, Dr. G.P. Malsekar. He was very surprised to see this. Third thing, I have got the "Ashoka Chakra" recognized in the Constitution as the insignia of the Government of India by the Indian Parliament. While doing all this I did not face much opposition from Hindus, Muslims, Christians and other members of Parliament. In this regard, I have discussed it point by point in the Parliament.

Has any one of the 28 countries participating in this third International Buddhist Conference done anything like this? I didn't stop doing this, so I have established a big college named

"Siddhartha" in the city of Bombay. Similarly, another college has been established in Aurangabad city on the way of Ajanta-Ellora. 2100 students are pursuing education in Bombay college and 500 in Aurangabad's college.

❑

# Buddha and his Dhamma

On a Saturday in March 1956, Babasaheb told Nanakchand Rattu, “Come early tomorrow morning.” Rattu came early on Sunday morning, when Babasaheb was writing the preface to this great book. Five minutes passed, yet Babasaheb's attention did not go towards Rattu. Seeing this, Rattu deliberately put both the books on the other side of the table. Then Babasaheb looked up and said, "You haven't gone home yet?" Rattu said, "I went home at midnight and came again this morning." Then Babasaheb was surprised and said, “I thought, you did not go home. Here the day passed and I went on writing. I didn't even move from here.” On hearing this Nanakchand's heart was overwhelmed.

Babasaheb Ambedkar worshiped the idol of Tathagat Buddha in the morning and sat down to write again. On March 15, 1956, he wrote the preface to the famous book "Buddha and his Dhamma" with his signature and gave it to Nanakchand Rattu for typing.

❑

# Buddha Jayanti

Today we all have gathered on the occasion of Buddha Jayanti. This birth anniversary has special significance. Since 1942, I have been demanding from the government that Buddha Jayanti should be celebrated. In between I was in the cabinet, then I was trying to get a public holiday declared on Buddha Jayanti, but my wish could not materialise. The then Home Minister Maxwell also wished that a holiday should be given on Buddha Jayanti, but due to the Great War, that wish also could not be successful. If Buddha Jayanti is declared a holiday then the help we get from the Muslims for the war will stop, they were in the same dilemma.

Later I joined the Congress cabinet. I had made the same demand even then. For this I followed Pandit Jawaharlal Nehru. Dr. Shyama Prasad Mukherjee, president of Mahabodhi Society also supported my demand. There is a holiday on the birthdays of 33 koti Hindu deities, so why not on Buddha Jayanti? I demanded from Mr. Nehru that out of all these holidays, one holiday should be reduced or one holiday should be extended. Pandit Nehru has great respect for Buddha. Coincidentally, the Nehru Government has declared a holiday on Buddha Jayanti from this year itself. But our Bombay government has not done this good work. The Bombay government is very cultured. Due to non-grant of leave by such government, the function of 5 pm is being held at 7:30 pm.

❑

# Buddham Sharanam Gachhami

When I was ten years old, my father was a Kabirpanthi monk. My father's house can be called the Dharmasana, similarly it can be called the Vidyasan. The way my father was a devotee of learning, in the same way he was a lover of religion. Reading Ramayana, Mahabharata in my childhood had a great impact on my mind. Father used to say- "We are poor, so there is nothing to fear. Why can't you be a scholar?"

I passed the matriculation examination, then the people of the chawl decided to welcome me with the help of Dada Keluskar. Father was against it. He said, "There is no need for felicitation. Welcoming a child will make him feel that he has become a leader. In the end, felicitation was carried out and Dada Keluskar presented a book named 'Buddha Charitra' in the felicitation. It was a different feeling after reading this book. Light filled up my mind. Ram, Sita, Lakshman went into exile. Abandonment of Sita at the behest of the washerman. Sixteen thousand wives of Krishna? These things sound terrible.

These things did not strike my conscience as true. But my study of Buddhism inspired me to study more. Even today my mind is influenced by Buddhism. I believe that only Buddhism can do good to the world?

My father used to say that we are poor. But our ambition should be bigger. Dronacharya of Mahabharata was poor. Dronacharya's wife used to mix millet flour in water and give it to her children in the form of milk. Karna came out of poverty. Great men are often born in poverty. My mind has started blooming like a flower after reading the character of Gautam Buddha.

I went to America for higher education. I studied Buddhism a lot there. What is Buddhism? I did a lot of study there to understand this and to calm the storm in my mind caused by the Buddha character. After much thinking, I understood the difference between Hinduism and Buddhism. My attachment to Buddhism is very old.

## What is Buddhism?

Gautam Buddha first got five disciples. These are called sages of Panchakoti. After having a total of sixty disciples, Buddha felt that he should order the disciples to go far and wide for propagating the religion. He said to the disciples, "You have mercy on them for the benefit of the Bahujan, for the happiness of the Bahujan. Tell the Dhamma for the welfare of the gods and humans. Which Dhamma is beneficial in the beginning, middle and end."

This religion is very imperative for the life of every human being. What is the soul like in other religions? Where does she live? this is not known to me. Is it the size of a thumb? or is near the heart? No one knows this. I haven't seen God till date. In Hinduism there is a place for God, the soul, but where is the place for man?

## Establishment of Buddhism

There is no discrimination in Buddhism, there is equality everywhere. In Buddhism, the idea is about how man should treat man, without considering God, the soul. Morality is everything in this religion. This is Saddharma. All other religions are false. Brahmins and parsons have created Hinduism. In Buddhism, there is no parson unlike in Christianity to achieve nirvana, and certainly no Brahmins who perform rituals and sacrifices to bring the soul to liberation. In this religion, conduct is essential for the welfare of man. That's why this religion is a public welfare religion.

## Who is the Teacher of Religion?

It has been 2500 years since the death of Gautam Buddha, yet this religion is propagating rapidly, while it has no ruler, no head. At the time of Mahaparinirvana, the disciple asked the Tathagat, "What will happen to this religion after you? You can make anyone a disciple of Dharma." Then he replied, "Dharma will be your yardstick in my absence. If you don't follow dharma, what is the use of dharma? Dharma practised with a pure mind will be your yardstick.

## When to Convert?

If not today then tomorrow we will have to convert. I have prepared the boat of change. Seven crore of our people are going to go to that shore by sitting in this boat. The strings of that boat are in my hands. That's why I am seriously contemplating all these things so that the boat full of people does not get caught in the storm, does not hit the rock, does not become weak and reaches the other shore safely. I will not start this work until I get a cock sure way.

Seeing my inclination towards Sikhism, Christian and Muslim communities are persuading following me. They are ready to give me seven crore rupees if I embrace their religion at this time. But I am getting seven crore rupees, because of this I am not going to push my brothers into the pit. The religion which suits my conscience and when I have complete faith, then only I will embark upon the boat of conversion and take my seven crore brothers safely to that shore and make their life stable. I have to raise the status of my poor, deprived, downtrodden untouchable brothers so high that everyone can become the ruler of princely states like Patiala and Hyderabad.

## Scripture

Now how will you continue to propagate Buddhism? We have to reflect about it. Three things are needed for the spread of religion-

1. Like the Bible of Christianity, making a scripture of Buddhism for the public, this is the first requirement.
2. The second requirement is to make necessary changes in the way of achieving the rules, goals and objectives of the Bhikshu Sangha.
3. The third need is to form Vishwa Buddha Seva Sangh.

I have mentioned above that the first and foremost need is to prepare the texts of Buddhism. There is a great need of Buddhist scriptures like Bible, Quran, Gita to keep the masses with them easily. In the absence of this type of scripture, the followers of Buddhism are facing a lot of inconvenience. Hindi Dhammapada did not fulfill this deficiency. The creation of every religion is based on faith. Hindi Dhammapada has not been composed on any basis, but an attempt has been made to generate faith through dry religious discussion. While composing the Bible of Neo-Buddhism, it should include Buddha character, Chinese Dhammapada, Buddha's dialogues and rituals and rites of events like birth, marriage, death. Language should not be neglected while composing such a book. The language of the book should be alive and sweet like coconut water. Reading this book should make a man sleepless and his thinking power should be awakened. The writing style of this book should be easy, simple, interesting, so that the curiosity of reading is generated in the reader.

I was busy writing a book on Buddhism for the last five years. That book should be published before my Dhamma initiation in the month of Vaishakh. It is for this purpose that I have come to Bombay. But due to a strange disease, I could not complete this book by writing it quickly. The book is written in English language having 700 pages. As a result, many of our people will have difficulty understanding. That's why I will get it translated into Marathi very soon. I could not go to Rangoon because of this work.

I am going to convert my religion in Bombay in coming October. Before that I am going to publish a book on Buddhism. Whatever is lacking in the religion of Tathagata, I am going to write it in detail in this book. In Buddhism, initiation is not given to the devotee. This has the opposite effect on the initiation of the Sangh. There is no complete make-up of the devotee's mind. But in my Buddhism the worshipers will be given Dhamma initiation. I am the author of a book before Dhamma initiation. Everyone must buy this book. Everyone has to answer some questions in this book, only then he will be able to enter Buddhism. Everyone has to wear white clothes while entering Buddhism.

## Change of Initiation Venue

I am well aware that the people of Bombay would be very envious if the place of initiation into Buddhism was changed to Nagpur. On the contrary, if the conversion ceremony were to take place in Bombay, how much outsiders would criticize us? We should consider this as well. That is, we should keep this feeling that all people are our own. The time has come for us to respect the wishes of outsiders. One thing we should keep in mind is that the first ceremony of Buddhist initiation will be held in Nagpur and the second ceremony will be held in Bombay. So there is no reason for the people of Bombay to be sad. Similarly, initiation programmes will be held at other places as well.

Where there will be a large number of Dhamma initiates, there will be an initiation ceremony. Such conversion ceremonies will take place at different places. I will personally be present at these events. I am going to publicly announce the date of Dhamma Deeksha through "Press Trust of India" i.e. this public announcement will also be published in "Prabuddha Bharat".

## I am reborn

Dhamma Diksha ceremony was held yesterday on the land of Nagpur to take and give Buddhist initiation, today a historic speech is being delivered regarding the initiation ceremony. Thoughtful people must be feeling somewhat strange that why did I take this work on my head? What is its need and what will be gained from it? But it needs to be analysed. Only after understanding this will the foundation of your work be strong.

Many people ask me why did you choose Nagpur city for this work? But the reason for choosing this place is completely different. Nag people propagated Buddhism in India. Evidence of burning these snake people is found in the Puranas. Agastya Muni could save only one snake from this fire. We are descendants of the same Nag. The settlement of Nag people was in and around Nagpur. Hence the city is called "Nagpur" which means "Village of Snakes." The name of the river flowing through the abode of snake people is also "Nag River". This is the main reason for choosing this place.

The poor need religion. The victims need religion. The poor lives on hope and the root of life lies in hope. What can happen when hope is lost? Religion makes a person optimistic. It gives a message to the victims that don't panic, your life will be hopeful. That's why a poor, suffering person remains attached to religion.

Man loves respect more than profit, profit is not dear. We fight for honour. We are trying to take man to perfection. Religion is very important for the progress of man. I know that a cult has emerged from the treatise of Karl Marx. According to them religion has no meaning. They don't care about religion. They want breakfast in the morning, in that they want pav, cream, chicken leg etc. Get a movie to watch and want a good night's sleep, everything is over then. This is their philosophy. I am not of these views, my father was poor. That's why I didn't get any such pleasure. No one would have spent life as painful as mine. How painful human life is amid wants, I know it well. I think economic progress is very important.

There is a difference between a man and an ox. The ox gets its fodder every day, similarly man also eats food. Yet there is a difference between the two. Man has body as well as mind. That's why both body and mind should be developed. The mind should be cultured.

The people of a country where there is no connection between food and cultured mind, say so. I have no intention of having any relation with the people of that country. Just as a man's body should be healthy while building relationships with others, similarly the mind should also be cultured. Otherwise, it would not be possible to say that mankind had been saved.

What is the basic premise of Buddhism? Tathagat Buddha has related that there is sorrow everywhere in the world. Ninety per cent of people are suffering from misery. To free the poor trapped in sorrow from sorrow is the prime task of Buddhism.

We'll go our way, you go yours. We have found a better way. This is the path to hope and prosperity. This path is not new. This path has not been brought from outside, rather it is the path of India. The principles enunciated by the Tathagat

Buddha are immortal, but the Buddha made no such claim. Such generosity is not found in any religion.

Bhadant Nagsen has ascribed three reasons for the destruction of religion. The first reason is that some religions are crude, there is no seriousness in the basic philosophy of that religion. That religion is temporary. The second reason is—if there are no able scholars to propagate the religion, then the religion gets destroyed. Knowledgeable people should tell the religion. Religion is defamed if one is not religious while debating with the opponents. The third reason is—the philosophy of religion remains limited to knowledgeable only. There are only temples and viharas for the common people.

Even if we become Buddhist, I will stick to political rights. I have full faith in this. What will happen after my death? I can't tell. A lot of work will have to be done for this movement. What if we accept Buddhism? If obstacles come, how will they be removed? What efforts have to be made for that? I have thought deeply about all this. Everything is full in my bale. I am fully aware of this. Whatever rights I have given, I have given them only for my people. The one who combined these rights will also combine those rights. I am the giver these rights and facilities. Then you must believe me. There is no fact in the propaganda of the opponents. I will prove it in the end.

❑

# Communism and Buddhism

Mr. President and Buddhist delegates,

The true method of life for everyone is Buddhism. Likewise, communism can be described as a way of life too. It is crucial for Buddhists to comprehend which of these two paths is superior. Particularly, the manner of life advocated by Buddhism is far more honorable than the approach advocated by communism. And it is crucial for Buddhists, especially the young, to fully understand this, as failing to do so will result in the destruction of the wisdom. The younger generation of Buddhists needs to be awakened by those having faith in Buddhism. Not only this, it should be explained to them why Buddhism is better than communism. Only then will Buddhism be able to survive.

What precisely results from understanding the mindset of Asian youth? They believe Karl Marx was the lone visionary and a brilliant person who enlightened human life. He should therefore be honoured first for this reason. We also need to consider what these young people think of the Buddhist monks.

I will not say much about it, but I will shed some light. In fact, these young people feel insecure if they dress like them, i.e., in bright yellow clothing. The monks ought to comprehend this attitude of youth. Similarly, the youth too should comprehend the significance of living a saintly life. A reforming strategy should also be developed on the question of "How can our Buddhism be better than communism."

To do this, one must comprehend where the objectives of communism and Buddhism differ. Knowing which path is eternal—Buddhism or Communism—is ultimately necessary. The path which is not eternal will lead you to the forest; rather towards anarchy, not perfection. Hence, going that route is improper. Although the road you have been instructed to take is sluggish and lengthy; but it is also reliable and secure. To achieve the goals you have set for yourself, I think it would be wise to take this course of action. The issue at hand is whether the short, winding road is preferable to the longer, straight one. Therefore, I will respond by saying that in life, there are frequently tiny roads with little distance to cover which prove deceptive.

## What is Communism?

What is the actual doctrine of communism? What are its constituents elements? By broadly assessing human life in this world, it becomes clear that exploitation occurs everywhere. And from this fundamental idea came communism. Due to the enormous wealth of the wealthy class, capitalists take advantage of the underprivileged by keeping them in pathetic living conditions. This is the starting point of Karl Marx. Marx frequently used the term "exploitation." The system that results in a class of people living in poverty and misery must be destroyed in order to end their suffering. According to Karl Marx, no one should keep their own private property with them. In the technical teams of Marx, owner of private property is an illegal/unauthorised owner of the production of labourers', labour force. Thus, he earns more money exploiting more labour of the labourers, but the labourers get nothing in return. The owner thus gets entire money. In this context, Marx has clear-cut opinion that why should the owner keep the extra money created by the worker's labour and who should own so much wealth? Marx argues that the rightful owner of the surplus wealth is the state, and hence, the state should keep it. Marx developed the concept of "the dictatorship of the proletariat" in relation to this philosophy. The implication is that, if running the state is necessary, only the class being exploited should do it, not the exploiting class. This is the fundamental tenet of Russian communist propaganda.

## Communism and Buddhism

Buddhist thought reveals that the issues raised by Marx were foreseen by the Tathagata Buddha a long time ago. Marx studied exploitation and discussed it. Similar to how Tathagat Buddha developed Buddhism 2500 years ago after perceiving the anguish of the impoverished and poor. The Buddha acknowledged that there is suffering in the world, despite the fact that he did not employ the word "exploitation." How true is the statement that the Buddha founded his faith on suffering? There are multiple uses for the term "sorrow." Rebirth or the cycle of rebirth is referred to as misery in some cultures. I do not agree with this viewpoint. In numerous places in the Buddhist teachings, sadness and destitution are compared. In nutshell, communism and Buddhism share a common foundation. I do not perceive any distinction between the two. Therefore, the Buddhist brothers do not need to look towards Marx led way to salvation. The firm basis of poverty is the subject of Tathagat's sermon Buddhist talk, "Dhamma Chakra Pravartana."

For this reason, I contend that everyone drawn to Karl Marx must read and pay attention to the teachings contained in the Dharma Chakra Pravartana, delivered by Tathagata. If one analyzes this "Sut-ta," he will undoubtedly comprehend my point of view. Buddha did not establish his religion on the principles of God, the soul, or the supernatural. He emphasized the reality of life. The fact that people are suffering is a fact. Thus, all of the fundamental tenets of communism were taught in Buddhism by Tathagat two thousand years prior to the birth of Marx.

Regarding private property, there are many parallels between Marx and the philosophy of Buddha. Being a means of private property production and to prevent exploitation, property should be owned by the government. As a result, the owner class will be unable to exploit the workers on the basis of owning private property. Marx adhered to this way of thinking. Now let us look at what the Buddha had to say about the Sangha and the guidelines Tathagat had established for the association of monks. No monk should own personal property, he has stated. Some sages must have made an error in judgment in this case. But it is true that the majority of sages do not possess private property. Sangh's laws and regulations on private property are so stringent that they are unheard of even in communist Russia. This topic has not yet been discussed.

## Why was the Bhikshu Sangha Established?

What was the motivation behind the creation of Tathagat Sangh? Why did he create this union in this manner? In this sense, a brief review of ancient history will be necessary. There were 'parivrajak' during the time while Tathagat Buddha was promoting Buddhism. A parivrajrak refers to an outcast who has left his home. There were conflicts between various tribes of forest dwellers during the time of the Aryans.

Some forest tribes were defeated and lost their support of life, driven out their homes. Consequently, they were these tribes led uncertain lives. Because they were nomads and so classified as "parivajrak". Gautam Buddha did great work of organising them. Buddha established guidelines for them;

and this guideline is known as the "Vinayapitaka". This rule prohibits the monk from owning any private property. Only seven items—a razor for shaving, a water bottle, a bowl for alms, three body-covering garments, and a sewing needle—can be owned by a monk. The importance of communism is to reject private property as well. Where else are more stringent guidelines available than those provided by Tathagat in Vinaypitaka? Nowhere! If a person or a Buddhist is drawn to the communist doctrine of abolishing the private property system, the Vinaypitaka of the Tathagata has previously developed this theory in great detail. The question that now emerges is how far the laws enshrined in Vinaypitaka can be applied to the entire society. Meaning, how much time, environment, and social evolution of human has happened? All it depends on this. But intellectualism does not stand in the way of abolishing private property. On the contrary, Tathagat made these rules thousands of year ago in the Buddhist Sangha.

Let us now analyse the other perspective on the aforesaid issue. Which method and tactics adopted to realize Karl Marx's or communism's objectives must be carefully considered. For the establishment of Communism, not a moment's consideration is given while killing opponents. The fundamental distinction between Buddhism and communism is this. The way of Tathagata Buddha is straightforward and true. It does not let the people to tread the incorrect path. He believes in sorting out any disputed issue using reason, morality, and compassion. Even Tathagat's adversaries have become believers in his religion. He believes that the best way to win someone over is with love and compassion rather than by using force. Buddhism and communism are distinct in this way. Buddhism forbids teaching violence, whereas communism promotes anarchy and loves violence. You may think that the Buddha's path is lonely and long, yet there is no question that it is complete, true and trustworthy.

Some of my friends are communists, and I frequently ask them questions; though they have not yet provided any satisfactory responses. Truly speaking they establish dictatorship of the exploited class through violence. They relinquish ownership of the landowners. I get 'no' response when I ask my communist pals if a dictatorship is an effective method to run the government. They claim that we dislike autocracy. I counter that if that is the case, why do you let a dictatorship run the government? They claim that a dictatorship of this kind is transitory. How long this brief period will be, I continue to bug. Twenty or thirty or forty or hundred years? They have no response to this. According to them, in the future, the dictatorship will fall out on its own. I follow up by inquiring what will happen if the regime of dictatorship ends. To whom will it succeed? Do people need government or not? They have been unable to provide an answer for this.

Let's now think about Tathagata's religion. The world's greatest lesson that Gautam Buddha imparts is to maintain a pure mind. There won't be a reformation of man or the world without a reformation of the mind. Where is the need for police or army to enforce good behaviour when a man accepts Buddhism and faithfully adheres to its principles? Your conscience is awakened by Tathagat's teachings, and you are prevented from straying from your path. Your discretion serves as the janitor. There cannot be a disruption or a riot when the mind is clean.

## Rationalism and Democracy

Buddhism has lent support to the democratic ideals. Buddhism means unadulterated democracy. Once the chief minister of King Ajatashatru went to Tathagata Buddha and said, "The King has to conquer the Vajjiyas." The Buddha said, "No one can defeat the Vajjiyas as long as they conduct their affairs properly on the right path." This is due to the fact that Gautama Buddha spoke in his sermons about democracy and the Vajji's democratic economic practices. The main point is that the Tathagat Buddha was a staunch supporter of democracy. The system that has been mentioned is very safe and advantageous system. If they desire to live with dignity in the world, I counsel all Buddhists to study and apply the teachings of the Tathagata as much as they can. I will certainly hold the monks responsible for any catastrophe that affects Buddhism. I get the impression that the monks are not adequately carrying out their duties. This is his conclusion.

I must say unequivocally that for propagation to succeed, education must constantly reflect on the eyes and ears of the underprivileged. How many years do children take to gain education?

Do not you take out your child out of school after sending him school just for one day? How will the children gain education then? Children should be sent to school every day for this reason. They should sit and study for 4-5 hours each day in school. Only when this takes place will children's minds be focused on learning and their level of knowledge progress. The same should be done for public education by monks. Additionally, moral education needs to receive specific attention.

If we manage to achieve even a tenth of what comprised Tathagat Gautam Buddha’s intelligenge, we will be able to contribute to society's welfare with kindness, fairness, and goodwill.

❑

# Final Speech

Sisters and Brothers,

Now is the time for the public to reflect carefully. Do the live portrayed in our religious books and the Constitution we drafted resemble each other in any way? What might be the cause if there isn't any similarity? We should pick between our Constitution and our religion. We Should either keep the Constitution or religion alive. Both cannot be merged or made to operate at the same time.

There are numerous sects in Hindu religion. The opinion of Shankaracharya is highly regarded among them. The most significant principle "Brahma Satyam, Jagat Mithya" is attributed to Shankaracharya. But it appears very insignificant and pointless in comparison to Buddhism's ultimate ideal.

The supreme obligation of the new converted Buddhists is to go to a Buddhist monastery every Sunday. They won't be able to learn more about their new religion if this doesn't happen. Buddhist monasteries need to be constructed in a number of locations for this. The monastery ought to have a gathering spot. The people of India should be assisted by Buddhist monks from nations such as Sri Lanka, Burma, Tibet, China, and others, who should come forward and collect money.

I met Mr. Dwarka Prasad, the former president (Adhyaksh) of Uttar Pradesh, this morning. He requested me to visit Jaunpur in December. Although I have promised to come, but no date has been fixed as yet. The massive community conversion programme in Jaunpur is currently under full preparation. On this occasion, thousands of members of the backward class from Uttar Pradesh's eastern districts would participate in Diksha, the initiation ceremony. These Dalits are still being abused by Hindus of the upper castes. By undergoing Buddhist initiation they are going to embrace the path shown by their forefathers.

## Buddhism Is Human Religion

Buddhism was established on a solid foundation. This religion was developed by humans. Other than this faith, no other religion is appropriate for the wellbeing of the people. We ought to be familiar with India's ancient history. The Aryans and the Nagas engaged in battle for the first time in India. Because the Aryans had horses, they were able to defeat the Naga, who are now known as Hindus. The first to accept Buddhism were the Nagas. Their efforts to popularise Buddhism were successful. However, the Aryans made numerous attempts to annihilate the Nagas. Mahabharata contains several instances where it is proved. Later, the Aryans disseminated the Brahmin religion, which gave rise to numerous flaws. The Chaturvarna system was established by the Brahmins. By dismantling it, Tathagat Buddha promoted equality and voiced his vehement opposition to this system. And in doing so, he founded the Bauddha Dharma. He disapproved of the Brahmins' Yagyas and ruled them invalid. The Brahmins began to act violently as a result, but Gautam Buddha stopped them by teaching non-violence. According to the Tathagata,

Buddhism is undifferentiated like the ocean. By pointing people in the correct direction, he attracted the oppressed of the day and preached compassion.

## Stigma of Untouchability

Hinduism has become an incurable disease, therefore we ought to convert to a new religion. Buddhism is the only worthwhile religion in my opinion. It doesn't encourage emotions of high vs low, caste vs creed, rich vs poor. The only way to ensure the welfare of the untouchables is to embrace Buddhism. Only by accepting Buddhism can the unfairness, prejudice, injustice, and evil practices that are pervasive in Hindu society be eradicated.

The untouchables of India will gain sympathy from the Buddhist nations like Burma, China, Japan etc. if we accept Buddhism and we shall be free from the exploitation of Hinduism forever. Why haven't these countries protested the injustice done to us up until this point? The reason behind this is that they believed it to be a infighting amongst Hindus. The aforementioned Buddhist nations will be our allies and co-partner in preventing us from being exploited if we accept Buddhism and Hindus continue to prevent us from enjoying equality, freedom, and fraternity.

Untouchability is an ugly stigma of the forehead of Hinduism. Because of this, there appears wickedness in the core of Hindu caste. Even though the untouchables adhere to all purity laws before visiting the Deities, yet they are not allowed entry into the Temples. The upper caste has a responsibility to abolish the caste system, discrimination, and untouchability. Why do we need to bear their body on our shoulders?

I would kindly request the untouchables to embrace a religion in which there is no distinction between people and they are all treated equally. The highest ideal in Buddhism is that people should be free to congregate in one area for being friends. After embracing Buddhism, everyone becomes equal, just as several rivers disappear into the ocean and lose their distinction from one another. Buddhism is advantageous to all of human society, not just the untouchables. Upper caste-Hindus ought to embrace this religion as well.

Other religions regard God as the universe's architect. Buddhism, however, does not adhere to this concept. Buddhism has a saying that there is suffering in the world, and that there is a cure to that suffering. Those paths should be considered for curing those sufferings. Hinduism bases its philosophy on conventions and traditions, and this tradition (Rudhi) originates from the Chaturvarna system. Buddhism has produced a large number of monks and nuns; "Theragatha and Therigatha" has information on them.

Hindus had the power to do justice, but they have till date continued to treat the untouchables unfairly. Untouchables should separate from Hinduism and prostrate themselves at Tathagata Buddha's feet. The newspapers have reported this false news that I was not permitted to enter the Pashupatinath Temple in Kathmandu. I never visit a Hindu temple. It would have been impossible for me to go to that temple even if I had been asked a hundred times to do so. A day ago, the Maharaja of Nepal had called my personal secretary to tell him that Dr. Saheb should not visit the temple. He added that Buddhists are not now permitted to access Hindu temples due to the current state of affairs. Previously, monks from Nepal, Sri Lanka, and India used to visit the temple, but they were forbidden to entre now. This would be mental torture for someone who does not believe in God. Additionally, insults will be directed at Hindu deities. The Buddhists should never visit Hindu temples. Buddhist monasteries treat everyone equally. Here, nobody impedes anyone.

Untouchables who desire to enter the temple by adhering to Hinduism are retrograde. What can I do in this situation if they wish to be offended and humiliated themselves? The Buddhists should not participate in this debate. We say this is in our daily prayer, "Natthi mein saranam ajja, Buddha mein saranam varam," which roughly translates to "I will take refuge in none other faith than Buddha". Why would someone who utters this desire to go to a Hindu temple? Temple entry in Kashi is a political gimmick. Dalits will not gain anything from this. Therefore, you should make it your primary goal to spread equality and brotherhood by accepting Buddhism.

❑

# The Last Message

Dr. Babasaheb Ambedkar has said, "It is a tremendous shame to be born in a nation when the populace's psyche is polluted by prejudice." Despite the fact that my work has been enormous, I have received both terrible criticism from all sides. I shall carry on with my work. To labour until I am dead is my motto.

"You go and tell my people that whatever I have done, I have done with great pain", Babasaheb stated to Nanakchand Rattu one day. "I have accomplished all of this by enduring pain and battling enemies all my life. To lead this convoy to this point, I have put in a lot of effort. No matter how many obstacles and crisis came in my path, this convoy must continue forward. If my fellow soldiers can't move this convoy ahead, it should at least remain where it is. But we shouldn't let our accomplishments up to this point go to waste. This is my last communication for my people."

❑

# Epilogue

As Dr. B.R. Ambedkar's autobiography draws to a close, we find ourselves in awe at the extraordinary journey of a man who overcame all obstacles and became a symbol of hope and liberty for countless people. The life narrative of Dr. Bhimrao Ramji Ambedkar is more than just a memoir; it is a legendary chronicle of the visionary's tenacity, fortitude, and indomitable spirit.

These chapters have demonstrated how Dr. Ambedkar's life was transformed by education. Through his intellectual pursuits, he transcended the limitations society had put on him and freed himself from the shackles of caste tyranny. He earned multiple degrees as a result of his unrelenting search for knowledge and the truth, which led to his illustrious educational tour overseas. It is impossible to overstate the value of education in his life. It gave him the confidence to oppose the existing status quo, criticise the repressive caste system, and fight for the rights of the oppressed.

Even today, Dr. Ambedkar's campaign against social injustice and caste prejudice has an impact, especially on young people, who are motivated to fight for their rights and the rule of law. Through his narrative we learned about the difficult circumstances the Dalit community faces and the pervasiveness of discrimination in all facets of their existence. His unwavering dedication to defending the rights and dignity of marginalised people acts as a beacon of hope, showing us that the fight for social justice is far from over.

The most significant aspect of Dr. Ambedkar's accomplishments was his crucial participation in the drafting of the Indian Constitution. As chairman of the Drafting Committee, he was instrumental in developing the fundamental document that governs the largest democracy in the world. The foundation for a country, enshrined in the Constitution, where every person is equal before the law and has a right to dignity and justice was built by his vision for an egalitarian society. His steadfast support for social reform, the reservation laws, and constant struggle for the abolition of untouchability have shaped modern India.

Dr. Ambedkar's legacy encompasses his teachings and philosophy in addition to his political and social accomplishments. In order to improve society, he emphasized the value of education, empowerment, and self-reliance. His words inspire generations, reminding us that true liberation lies not only in political freedom, but also in the liberation of the mind. Indelible impressions of his plea for the abolition of caste and the establishment of a society founded on the ideals of liberty, equality, and fraternity can be seen throughout his autobiography.

We are obliged to consider the ongoing importance of his life and ideas as we come to the close of this journey through his autobiography. His hardships, triumphs, and unrelenting dedication to social justice serve as a sobering reminder that the campaign against prejudice and inequality is a never-ending task. We must continue to be inspired by his life and work, emulating his attitude of compassion, fortitude, and unyielding resolve.

Let's work to create a society where everyone, regardless of caste, creed, or gender, enjoys equal rights and access to socio-political empowerment, education, and healthcare. Let's fight against repressive structures that support prejudice and seek to create a society that is more fair and inclusive.

The autobiography of Dr. B.R. Ambedkar is proof of the resilience of the human spirit and the ability of a person to make a difference. It stands for the strength to overcome misfortune, the quest for knowledge and justice, and the unflinching dedication to the advancement of humanity. May this effort serve as a constant source of inspiration, reminding us of the unfinished business of building a society that upholds the values of equality, justice, and dignity for every individual.